FIND HIM & KILL HIM

CODY J. THOMPSON

Black Rose Writing | Texas

ISBN: 978-1-68513-417-4
PUBLISHED BY BLACK ROSE WRITING
www.blackrosewriting.com

Printed in the United States of America
Suggested Retail Price (SRP) $19.95

Find Him and Kill Him is printed in Garamond Premier Pro

*As a planet-friendly publisher, Black Rose Writing does its best to eliminate unnecessary waste to reduce paper usage and energy costs, while never compromising the reading experience. As a result, the final word count vs. page count may not meet common expectations.

For Lemmy Rose.
Born to lose.
Live to win.

FIND HIM & KILL HIM

CHAPTER 1

Mitch knew the fireworks were about to begin. Though, being only on the business end of 14, his young mind couldn't comprehend the magnitude or reality of what was to come. Or, just how much his life would change on that Memorial Day in 2006.

Once the sun fell beyond the horizon, everyone at the block party on Whippoorwill Glen knew it would be time for the light show in the sky. The sun had already begun its inevitable descent allowing the desert sky to burst on fire. Its remaining rays, fighting to ignite everything in sight, burned through the puffy clouds transforming the dusk sky into what resembled a bowl of rainbow sherbet. Oranges mingled with brilliant purples, and, when the rays hit just right, sent gorgeous greens that peek-a-booed from behind the clouds.

Mr. Burky and his son, Moe, had begun preparations for that evening's fireworks show hours ago. This wasn't your typical cul-de-sac fireworks show, Mr. Burky always made sure of that. Each year, he would do whatever it takes to top his previous year's performance. Though the show, if you could call it that, two years prior, had become the easiest to beat. How could anyone in the neighborhood forget the time that the entire stack of mortars, which Mr. Burky hadn't properly secured to the ground, tipped onto their sides, effectively giving Mrs. Parker's driveway its own intimate showing. A barrage of glitter, fire and colorful sparks bounced off her garage door, driveway and roof transforming her home into the largest party popper you'd ever seen. To this day, people still consider it a miracle he didn't burn her house down to the studs. That's because Burky didn't buy your standard fireworks. You know the ones, the mass-packs sold in wire baskets at the grocery store or at a janky roadside stand. Memorial Day was special on Whippoorwill Glen. Your typical Black Cats, snakes, whirly dos and rock fountains just wouldn't cut it on this day of all days. Those are always fun for the kids. But Burky's choice in explosives, those were the real deal. The fireworks typically seen at amusement parks and carnivals. The *big* boys that fly high above even the tallest house on the block, sending sparks of all different colors into the night sky. It was a serious fire hazard in the dry, Bakersfield landscape. Though it wasn't legal, Burky and the rest of the neighborhood weren't concerned about being stopped or ticketed, him being a member of the fire department and all.

Every year on Memorial Day, the families that lived on Whippoorwill Glen gathered at the end of the cul-de-sac to mark the return of summer. Dirty folding tables, masked with gingham patterned tablecloths which lined the blacktop, each filled with different bowls and platters of more food than any party needed. Mrs. Parker, a recent widow, even came out of hiding on this special day to serve, what she considered, her famous macaroni and potato salads. Though, Mitch remembers his mother whispering to his father that she suspected both were store bought. No one cared, they would devour each massive bowl all the same. Soft rolls graced their own serving trays, next to countless neon, plastic bowls overflowing with every flavor of potato chip one could imagine. Dips of all kinds accompanied the potato chips, the containers sweating from the heat, as adults continued to stir the layer of grease that settled on the top, mixing them so no one would notice. The headliner at each Memorial Day block party were of course the dueling grills that were rolled into the street. At the far end of the cul-de-sac, butted up against the curb, four roll away grills pumped flames and smoke into the air. Everyone watched with hungry eyes as Mr. Graham, Mrs. Stevens and Mr. Looney frantically flipped burgers and hot dogs to keep up with the hungry masses.

Mitch Graves blazed through the folding chairs and tables on his shiny, silver BMX. His baggy blue jeans and oversized zip up hoodie flapped in the minimal breeze as he tore through the crowd of neighbors, stopping just in front of the table that held the sizzling burger patties and over-charred hot dogs. He skidded to a stop, fishtailing his back wheel as he did, stopping just before crashing into the table and sending all that food to the dirty blacktop. Grabbing a hot dog with his bare hands, he dropped it into a bun before drizzling it with bright, yellow mustard and shoving it into his mouth.

"Hey, slow down, kiddo," Mrs. Graves, Mitch's mother shouted over the crowd. She jumped to her feet from her folding chair. "You almost crashed and took the food with you! Be more careful, OK?"

Amidst the party goers were Mitch's parents, resting in folding beach chairs. Mrs. Graves, a mother of the year nominee by the looks of it, held a plate of food in one hand, Mitch's baby sister, Myrna, in the other. It was as though having her hands full was second nature. Mr. Graves remained in his chair, an oversized bite of a much too well-done cheeseburger filling his mouth, making it hard–or at least impolite–To speak. He nodded his head in agreement regarding his wife's warning to their son. Mitch, a half eaten hot dog in hand, peddled to his parents, resulting in yet another audible skid of his bike tires.

"I wasn't going to hit the table," Mitch said with a tinge of attitude in his voice. He took another bite. "I know what I'm doing."

"Keep it below the speed limit, would ya?" Mrs. Graves asked, settling back into her chair. "We don't need you taking out any of the older folks who can't see or hear you coming."

"Hey mom, Can I have a soda?"

"How many have you had today?"

"I don't know," Mitch knew. Every kid always knows.

"If you say that *you don't know*, I'd say you've had too many. Have a bottle of water instead."

Aww man, Mitch thought to himself, and the look on his face told the story his lips kept private. He scanned the group of neighbors, all appearing to settle in as the sun continued to fall behind the horizon. Each guest holding their respective plates of BBQ and snack foods, mingling with one another. Their voices were so loud, you almost couldn't hear the radio set on one table playing top 40 hits.

"Say mom," Mitch cut in after swallowing the last bite of lukewarm hot dog. "Do you mind if I take a ride out to the train tracks?"

"Mitch, honey. It's going to be dark soon. The fireworks are going to start."

"I'll be back in time."

"I don't know that I want you hanging around those train tracks by yourself. Especially at night."

"Oh, come on hun," Mr. Graves said, taking a sip from a weeping can of cold, yellow beer. "He's a young boy. Let him get himself into a little trouble. He can't hide behind you forever."

"Thanks for having my back, Stan," She muttered with a roll of the eyes.

"Go ahead, son," Mr. Graves said, motioning him away with his right hand. "Just be back before the show starts. You made me lug this chair down the street for you, so you'd better use it."

"Thanks, Dad!" Mitch shouted through a wide grin. He began peddling away just as his mother's voice caught his ears again.

"Mitch, see if Moe will go with you!" She looked towards her husband. "You can let him go, but I can still be protective, got it?"

Mitch pedaled his way to the staging area where Mr. Burky and his son, Moe, made preparations for the upcoming fireworks show. Moe was the same age as Mitch, though by his size, most people mistook him for a much older boy. His large body encapsulated Mitch and his thin frame in shadows. Like his father, Moe was strong, his life path blazed for him by a family legacy of firefighters. It was something that made their family beam with pride. So much so, Moe was wearing his signature Bakersfield Fire Department t-shirt, like he did most days.

"Hey, Moe," Mitch yelled, stopping his bike to the side of the fireworks mortars. "Grab your bike, I wanna ride out to the train tracks before the show starts."

"Mitch, come on, man." Moe said, wiping sweat from his brow. "I've gotta help my dad set up."

"Dude come on," Mitch lowered his voice to a whisper. "I added a couple new nudie mags to my collection out there." He winked at Moe.

"No shit," Moe replied, showing a newfound interest in this possible dusk bike ride. "Where the hell did you get those?"

"Mr. Looney left his garage door open," Mitch whispered, looking over his shoulder to ensure no one was listening. "I saw them inside his recycling bin. I guess Mrs. Looney found his stash again."

"They any good?" Moe asked under his breath.

"What do you think?" Mitch asked, looking at his friend out of the top of his eyes.

"Shit," He whispered. He lifted his voice as he continued, "Hey dad? Can I ride out to the tracks with Mitch before the show starts?"

Mr. Burky was a massive man, towering over everyone in the neighborhood. His visible muscles burst through his t-shirt, showcasing different tattoos that he had collected over the years. Like his son, they could always find Burky in some sort of fire department gear. A walking billboard for public service. Tonight's choice? A dark blue dad hat with the local department's logo embroidered into the front.

"Absolutely not," He shouted with a deep sternness in his voice. "This tradition matters, Moe. How many times do I have to tell you that? Besides, one day this entire tradition will be *yours*. For now, it's *ours*. You've gotta put the work in, just like I do."

"Sorry Mitch, no can do," He said, shrugging his shoulders. "Let's go out tomorrow, OK?"

"Yeah, OK," Mitch said, defeat in his young voice. "Probably a good idea for you to help, anyway. We don't need another accident like a few years ago."

"Hey, keep your voice down," Moe instructed. "My dad will kick your ass if he catches you talking about that."

"Hey Mr. Burky," Mitch shouted, his feet already on the pedals, picking up speed.

"Don't forget to secure the mortars this year!"

Mr. Burky chased Mitch towards the end of the cul-de-sac before slamming his feet to a stop.

"Yeah, ride away you little smart ass!" He shouted. His angry face soon turned to a laugh as he shook his head slightly. He knew he'd never live that mistake down.

Past the curb at the end of the street, there was a cutout in the fence that led to a sprawling field just outside the neighborhood. The field stretched far into the Bakersfield desert, littered with nothing more than dead weeds in the shade of minimal trees sticking up like bad teeth from the dried dirt. Way off in the distance, far enough it was hard to see, sat a set of old train tracks. These tracks clearly hadn't seen activity in what Mitch and other kids figured was decades. Not only from the bends in the steel but also from the dilapidated, filth covered train cars that remained rotting in the desert sun on those old, forgotten tracks. Mitch pedaled his way through the dirt and weeds, picking up speed headed towards the railway. The air was growing cold, so he knew he didn't have long. But he loved hanging out in those train cars. And, as he'd sworn before, not only because the promise of some fresh adult magazines awaited him.

CHAPTER 2

Three train cars sat abandoned in the expansive field neighboring Mitch's street. Two rail cars–one red and one black–pushed against one another. Down the tracks a bit sat another railcar, its rusted blue paint dimming more and more as the sun and elements beat down upon it. The cars were a haven for kids of all ages and had been for what seemed like forever. Different generations of kids had used the rail cars' secrecy as a place to make out, smoke and drink or to take part in some general non-chaperoned shenanigans and hijinks. Each car once had massive rolling doors on either side, though they'd all disappeared some time ago, allowing for the fresh air to blow through. This made the antique, musty smell that mixed with rust quite minimal. Different graffiti decorated the inside and outside of each of the cars, covered by more and more years of vandalism.

Mitch skidded out in the dirt just before the red car. A plume of dust and dirt kicked into the air as he dismounted, dropping his BMX hard onto the dirt floor. Planting his hands into the cold steel of the car, he pushed himself up, crawling inside. This specific car was the one Mitch liked most. He rarely saw others hanging about at the train tracks anymore, so, most days, he and Moe could call it their own. They always seemed to discuss grandiose plans to clean the car inside and out, making it a true hang out spot. Almost like their own clubhouse. Though, the idea of fixing the place up, making it their own, just so some older teens or drifters could show up and destroy all their work seemed to keep their plans at bay. Regardless, this was where Mitch kept his stolen nudie magazine collection. Obviously, keeping them at home wasn't an option. Not a chance. It wasn't much, but for the 12-year-old mind, any look into the world of the taboo was plenty to tantalize the senses. Most of the magazines he had stored inside the train car he stole from his neighbor, Mr. Looney. It was like a never-ending cycle with him; it seemed. Buy a bunch of magazines, get caught with them, and toss them into the recycling bin. It didn't take long for Mitch and Moe to figure this cycle out, so they took it upon themselves to check his recycling each Wednesday before the trash trucks arrived. Just last week, Mitch got lucky, adding six new editions to his ever-growing library.

The inside of the train cars were filled with junk and trash that no one would ever need. Different steel barrels, pallets and wooden crates that probably held milk bottles or something from way back when. It elated Mitch when he found a small opening on one of the wood crates; the perfect housing for his growing magazine collection. How no one had found these and stolen them was something he never understood. Though, anytime they returned to the cars to find them still intact and in place, it was like discovering them again for the first time. The immature excitement that lived deep inside a pre-teen's brain was easy to unlock, if you had the right attributes.

He sat, his back pressed into the steel wall of the train car. He pulled the wooden crate from the shadows, settling in with his new reading material. From the inside of his pocket he removed a lollipop. Unwrapping it, he tossed the paper onto the floor, flipping through one magazine he hadn't yet explored.

"*Damn*," He said to himself slowly, twisting the magazine to its side. "Just gorgeous."

Just as he settled in and lost himself in the pages, Mitch was startled out of his stupor by a loud, hollow sounding bang. His body jumped, as he curled into himself. The loud thud sounded close. So close, in fact, it seemed to have occurred right beside him. The air around him fell silent, becoming almost thick. His nerves shook inside his body, as his breath shuddered. After a moment of silence, another loud bang. Followed by another. He looked to his right, realizing this sound–whatever it might be–was clearly coming from the railcar that sat butted up to his. Slowly, he crawled on all fours to the opening of the car, carefully dropping his body to the dirt. Remaining crouched, he moved towards the second railcar. With just his fingertips gracing the edge of the flooring, he glanced inside to see what might make the loud, banging noises. His body quivered, unsure of what he might find. A helpless animal, maybe? He hoped he wasn't about to come face to face with a possum, or even worse, an angry skunk that might spray him.

Inside, coming from the shadows of the far left wall, Mitch saw legs. *Human* legs. Wrapped in dark blue running pants, the feet adorned with white athletic sneakers. The legs tremored, as the right leg rose into the air before crashing into the cold steel over and over. His eyes were as wide as he could ever remember as he watched the mystery person writhe, clearly in extreme pain, fighting off something—or someone—that Mitch couldn't see. If this *was* an animal, he wanted no part of it. He couldn't see the body attached to those legs, but he was certain the person was bigger than him. He wouldn't stand a chance against whatever predator hid just a few feet away.

As Mitch stood he took a step back from the car but before he knew it, he was on his back. His small body skid across the dirt, his arms in front of him to fight off whatever—or whoever—took him down. He felt an immense weight upon his chest, followed by a hot breath that smacked his face. He shook his head and whimpered, as tears filled his closed eyes.

"Who the *fuck* are you?" A deep, gravel filled voice asked.

When he opened his eyes, they landed and focused first on the largest knife he'd ever seen, hovering just inches above his quivering chest. He followed the knife to the hand, then down the man's arm to see who had tackled him to the ground.

Dressed in what looked like old, tattered rags, his long, stringy brown hair poured over his sun-bleached face, which was covered by an unkempt beard. His beady eyes burned with rage as they pierced through Mitch's entire being, as though they were looking to drag his soul from his body and tear it to shreds.

"Please," Mitch stuttered, pressing his feet deep into the dirt, trying to push himself from the attacker. "Let me go!"

The man spun the knife in his hand, now holding the blade long ways across Mitch's chest. He pressed the blade into the young boy's neck. With the cold blade pressed against Mitch's chin, lifting his head back into the dirt. Mitch could feel the chill of the knife, the blade, sending shivers through his body.

"Who the fuck sent you?" The man asked through gritted teeth.

"Who *sent* me?" Mitch choked out, his words trading places with coughs. "I'm only 14. I-I brought myself here."

The man lifted the knife from Mitch's throat, keeping his left hand on his shoulder, holding him to the ground. He held the knife at his side, as he slowly lifted himself first to his knees, then stood above the boy. Mitch kicked his feet into the ground, pushing himself away from the man, who appeared like nothing more than a drifter. A random homeless man who had found his way to Mitch's beloved hang out spot. He tried to get to his feet, but eventually fell to his ass, thanks to the extreme trembling affecting his legs.

"You shouldn't be here, little boy," The drifter said, returning the knife to a holster on his hip. "Who are you? Where did you come from?" His eyes shot across the landscape, searching for anyone else who may sneak up on him.

"I-I," He stuttered. "I'm no one!" He held his hands in front of his body, bracing for an attack he felt was inevitable.

"What the fuck are you doing here, little kid?" He grabbed him by the collar again.

"I-I hang out here all the time!" Mitch shouted. "What, what did you do to, to that man?"

"What man?"

"*That* man! The man in the train car!"

"Oh, him," The drifter said with a laugh. "You don't need to worry about him. Well, not *anymore*."

"Is he?" Mitch began, attempting to look around the drifter. "Is he *dead*?"

The drifter looked over his shoulder towards the open railcar, an inquisitive look on his face. He took a few steps, leaning into the shadows to inspect the inside. To see what was left of the man.

"Uh," He finally said, "Well, he is *now*."

"Oh, my god!" Mitch screamed. "You *killed* him!?"

"Hey, hey!" The man shouted through whispers, rushing back to Mitch. "Keep your voice down, little boy. We don't know who might be milling about."

"But you did. You, you killed that man!"

"Yes," The man finally admitted, kneeling to Mitch. "I killed that man. I guess you caught me."

"But why?"

"It's something you're too young to understand, little boy," He whispered, eyes glaring deep into Mitch's. "Now, tell me I don't have another little problem on my hands."

"What do you mean? You mean *me*?"

The drifter slowly nodded his head. The look on his face did the speaking for him. This was no time for jokes. He meant business.

"Where do you live, kid?"

Mitch tried to withhold that information, but when the knife made its way back into view, he knew he had little argument. At only 14, there was plenty he didn't know. But, he was certain of a few things; if he didn't spill the beans, whatever happened to that poor man inside the cold, steel box could soon happen to him. And, if he gave someone else's address, this man could go looking for the wrong people. He might put someone else in danger. Even though he didn't want this man to know where he lived, he couldn't put someone else in this man's path. Besides, the only other address he could recite by heart was Moe's. And you don't always think straight with the cold, steel blade of a knife pressed to your throat. In times like this, you tend to lose yourself. So, without giving his official address, he explained where he lived within the neighborhood in the distance behind him. At that moment, with his nerves on high alert, he probably couldn't speak his own name, let alone his address.

"Now, you run along. And we agree, right? You *saw nothing* here. And if something jogs your memory, well," He sucked air through his teeth. "Let's just say you don't want me making any unnecessary house calls. Got it?"

The drifter turned his back to Mitch, hurrying to the opening of the black car. In one quick motion, he hoisted himself up and inside. Mitch stood quietly for a moment, before going against his better judgment and taking a couple footsteps in the wrong direction. He stopped just a few feet from the opening, thinking, if the drifter came back at him with another attack, maybe he could make a run for it.

"Hey," Mitch shouted into the opening of the car. His voice, echoing loudly against the steel walls. "Why are you letting me go?"

"Would you prefer I *not* let you go?" The man said from inside.

Mitch couldn't see what he was doing, though he heard more thuds, less intense this time. More like the sound he'd remembered when his dad grilled steaks at home, dropping the cold, raw meat onto a cutting board. Wet thuds of meat against liquid.

"No, it's not that," Mitch said, peering into the shadows. "Why didn't you kill me?"

The man remained silent for a moment. Even the noises from inside stopped. Mitch figured he must be pondering the question. He then figured it was probably the second mistake he'd made that day at the tracks. *Why did I ask that?* He thought to himself. He closed his eyes, bracing for whatever attack may come. But, it startled him as the man didn't come for him. No, he merely answered the question, to Mitch's pleasant surprise.

"It's not what I do," He said, his voice bouncing off the walls of the car.

"But you killed him? Who is he?"

"Look," The man shouted, returning from the shadows, leaning out the side of the opening. "I said you could go as long as you keep your trap shut. So, move along, kid. Don't make me second guess this and *definitely* don't make me regret it."

"What did you mean, killing me isn't what you do?"

"My *god* you ask a lot of questions, kid. You're making me uncomfortable. It's just…It's not what I do. I don't kill kids."

"So, if you don't kill kids, doesn't that make me safe? You know, to stay here?"

The man's face washed over with confusion. *The nerve of this little shit,* he thought.

"It's not what I do," He said before lowering his voice to a whisper. "*Yet.*" He flashed the knife again before returning to the shadows.

"Wait!" Mitch shouted into the shadows. "Can I see?"

The man returned to the minimal light, kneeling down in front of the boy. He let out a deep sigh.

"What is your problem, kid? You've got some sort of complex? Why do you want to see what I've done? If you've seen one dead body, you've seen thousands," He said with another sigh. "Haven't you ever seen a dead body before?"

"No," Mitch said, rubbing the back of his head. He continued as a creepy smile washed over his young face. "But I'd like to."

CHAPTER 3

This sort of sickening interest had never crossed Mitch's thoughts before now. Leering at a dead body and all. Seeing another human being who was alive only 20 minutes ago, now, his limbs sprawled out every which way. All the life had poured from his body, leaving nothing more than a memory behind. A cooling corpse in the evening, desert air. Whereas most kids of Mitch's age might watch the movie *The Mighty Ducks* and beg their parents for a new hockey stick, Mitch found himself deeply interested in something much more sinister. Being this close to death sparked something inside of his young mind. And for reasons he wasn't sure of, he wanted to be a part of what was inside that railcar.

"Why in the hell do you want to see a dead body?" The man asked, kneeling just inside the freighter. He held the knife, the tip pressed under his chin as he spun the handle in his right hand.

"I don't know. I'm 14. I'm *annoying*. At least that's how everyone treats me. I guess I'm just curious."

The man pondered this for a moment. Could he trust this kid? What was the kid really after? If he gave him a peek into his handiwork, would the kid keep his word and stay quiet about this encounter? So many questions flooded his mind like a tornado ripping through a neighborhood. Too many questions, too little time to think.

"Fine," The drifter finally said, nodding his head slightly. "Under *one* condition. I let you take a peek, you keep your little trap shut about everything you've seen and heard today. Deal?"

"Deal!" Mitch agreed, almost too quickly.

The drifter took the knife into his left hand, extending his right hand down to Mitch. Mitch locked his hand into the drifters as he pulled him into the train car. The man's hand was cold–ice cold. As though, at that moment, Mitch was holding hands with death himself. It sent a shiver through his body, but the excitement surrounding the situation made the shivers subside just enough to keep going. Coming from the shadows were the legs Mitch had already seen. The dark blue pants, the white sneakers. Somehow, even in the shadows, the legs now looked different to him. He could tell immediately that there was no life left in them. The way they laid, both feet pointed inwards at one another, he thought they looked like doll's legs. Lifeless, boneless, flopping doll legs.

He took a few slow steps forward, peering around a large, wooden crate, hoping to see the dead body without having to get too close. The sunny day had come on and gone, making way for twilight, and the minimal moonbeams that poured through the cracks and breaks in the steel gave just enough for his young eyes to see. The closer he got, the more the body came into focus. First, he could see the waist. His eyes followed up the torso, noticing a matching dark blue runners jacket, lined with white trim. Dark stains covered the front of the jacket, a sort of black, oily looking liquid. He noticed the liquid had poured from two puncture wounds on the chest. Next to the body, the right arm dangled as lifeless as the feet and legs, the hand in a sort of claw. The fingers now stuck in time from a fight to the death. The palm, decorated in wet, bloody gashes as the man had tried to fight off the blade of his attacker.

As he took another step closer, his nose was met with an odor. A musty, old smell thanks to the train and its remaining items mixed with the copper scent of fresh blood. Another step closer, the rest of the man came into focus. He could see the man's face lit just barely by the moonlight fighting its way into the container. Stuck in the shadows, Mitch could make out the face, its mouth, gaping wide. The tongue sitting just inside, almost perched upwards towards the roof of his mouth. His eyes, wide open, locked in a state of fear. They seemed almost painted on, as they continued to dry in the breeze that flowed through the container. The dried, terrified eyes stared into the distance at everything and nothing all at once. Just under the low hanging jaw, Mitch could see the man's neck. It had been slashed wide open, crimson liquid pouring from the massive gash stretching almost ear to ear. Mitch couldn't help but feel the body looked more like a mannequin than a man. Some sort of creepy prop used in those old horror movies that played late at night on Channel 11. He knelt down close to the dead body, reaching out his right hand towards the corpse's lifeless, emotionless face.

"Don't!" The drifter shouted, grabbing Mitch by the shoulder. "Don't touch *anything*. Move back."

"I just want to feel–"

"I *know* what you're doing," He cut in. "Just don't."

"Is he cold?"

"He will be. Soon enough."

Mitch knelt down again to admire the body. This time, keeping a clearer distance from the carnage before him.

"How does it feel?" Mitch asked, his eyes locked on the body.

"How does what feel?"

"When you stick the knife into him. When you kill him."

The container grew eerily quiet. The drifter taking slow steps towards Mitch. Unable to resist, Mitch again reached out just one finger towards the dead man's face. Slowly he pushed his scrawny arm outward, he was so close to feeling death for the first time when–

BANG!

Mitch pulled his arms into his body, falling back onto his ass. Then again–

BANG! BANG!

"Oh, shit!" Mitch shouted, rising to his feet.

"What the hell is that? Fireworks?"

"I told my parents I'd be back before the fireworks started. I've gotta go."

Mitch turned past the drifter, dashing towards the opening of the train car. Before he could jump out, the drifter shoved his skinny body against the wooden crate. He extended the knife over Mitch's throat.

"You remember our deal, kid. I let you come in and nose around, you keep that mouth of yours *shut*. You got it?"

"I-I got it," Mitch drooled out, the knife pressed into his flesh. "I promise I won't say a word to anyone."

The drifter finally relaxed the knife, then let go of Mitch's hoodie, allowing him to jump down. He landed in the hard dirt and immediately rushed to his BMX. Lifting it from the dirt, he turned back to the drifter, who stood in the wide opening of the car, watching Mitch's every move.

"Is this where you always come to do this?" Mitch asked.

"What do you mean by that?"

"Is this where you come to, you know, *kill?*"

"I go wherever my business takes me. Remember that, this is *my* business. Not yours. You'd best just forget this ever happened, kid."

"What are you going to do with him?"

"I said forget this ever happened!" The drifter screamed, jumping from the train car, knife in hand. "Now get the fuck outta here!"

Mitch mounted his BMX and hightailed it back to the neighborhood. He pedaled as fast as his feet could take him, illuminated by the bright, beautiful sparks that showered down from above.

CHAPTER 4

Mitch didn't sleep a wink that night. Not that he couldn't because of reasons one might expect. Most would imagine a little boy would be haunted by what he'd seen. Dreams taken over by dancing corpses and skeletons coming for him in the night. Though, every time he closed his eyes, he wasn't confronted by visions of dead bodies, their throats slit ear to ear, bleeding their life into the open, summer air. It was because of excitement. He found himself excited by what he had seen and witnessed. At first, he felt odd by his newfound wonder with death. He knew it was taboo, not something that friends, teachers and family would accept. Much like the nudie magazines he'd lifted from Mr. Looney's recycling bins, it was an excitement he would need to hide from others. Hide from everyone, except the drifter. He realized he never got that man's name, nor did he know if he'd ever encounter the killer again. But as he laid in bed, eyes wide open with wonder, he hoped that in due time he would.

Sleepless nights, though, have their drawbacks. When late-night Mitch transformed to morning Mitch, it was that version who then felt like death. His eyelids hung low, his body slumped as he moved. Moving slowly to get ready that morning not only resulted in his mother shouting down the hall at him endlessly to pick up the pace, it also meant getting to school later than he preferred. Not that Mitch enjoyed being at school. Most 14-year-old boys in fact don't enjoy their time in the classroom. Aside from the couple of do-gooders in each class, kids were too preoccupied with the extra curricular to worry about schoolwork. He definitely never wanted to arrive on campus early for academic purposes. No early visits to the library, no extra credit projects in the works. It wasn't what he wanted to do early at school; it was who and what he wanted to avoid. And that was Bobby and his cronies. The vile, older bullies who not only loved, but *lived* for tormenting the younger, male student body. Mitch, in particular it seemed, who'd recently become their preferred target.

Mitch and Bobby had known each other for years, growing up in the same neighborhood and playing on little league teams together. Bobby was a year older than Mitch, and for many years, they got along well. It wasn't until Bobby had transferred to Junction High School, leaving Mitch behind in Middle School, that the two lost their old, friendly ways. When he started hanging out with all the older kids who spent their time causing trouble and picking fights, naturally, it wasn't long before Bobby joined on to help create chaos. Big for his age, Bobby could fit in with upperclassmen and no one batted an eye. Being familiar with Bobby was all it took for Mitch to become a target of his torment. With most bullies, it's usually familiarity and lack of self confidence that brings out the worst in them. And boy did Mitch bring out the worst in his old pal.

Junction High was the largest school in the district. Its outdoor campus comprised building after building in long rows stretching the prodigious property. Each building housed classrooms in rows, the classes broken down by the category of the subjects taught within. The science row, the math row and so on. In the middle of campus was an immense grass area where students ate lunch, took part in different school activities and congregated before and after class. The far end of the campus had an enormous blacktop parking lot which butted up against a wall of handball and basketball courts. Not only was this the area used for drop off each morning, but the handball courts were also the favorite hangout for students wanting to sneak a smoke before and between periods. A perfect place for kids to hide from security guards cruising the grounds on mountain bikes. Some of the main offenders, of course, were Bobby and his jerkoff pals. When Mitch got dropped off late that morning, he knew he was in for an unpleasant encounter. He could feel it deep within his bones, his primal instinct kicking in like a baby deer left alone in a clearing.

"Are you going to be OK today?" Mrs. Graves asked, slowing the car to a stop in the school's parking lot. "You don't look like yourself."

"Yeah. I'll be OK. I'll grab a soda from the cafeteria before first period."

"A soda? For breakfast? Mitch," She said, shaking her head.

"I didn't get a lot of sleep last night. Hopefully, it'll help wake me up."

"Tonight you're going to bed early, you hear me?"

"Fine, mom," He said with a sigh, opening the passenger door.

"Have a good day, sweetheart. Try not to fall asleep in class."

"Mom, come on," He said, leaning into the car. "I'll be fine, I promise."

"Ok, ok, Mr. Attitude," She said. She raised her voice. "I *love* you!"

Mitch shot a smile back to her. Most freshman boys wouldn't be caught dead telling a parent they loved them in public. That could land you in hot water for your entire high school career. And Mitch needed no more reason to fear for his life at Junction High. Not with Bobby and his gang lurking around. With his head lowered, he walked with a serious pace through the parking lot, hoping to sneak his way by the handball courts. There was a subtle scent of cigarette smoke in the air, so his senses warned him the crew of bullies weren't far. The side of the gymnasium was *so close*, he could almost smell the dirty gym socks and sweat covered wrestling mats emanating from within. Almost home free. Just as he unclenched himself, he heard that obnoxious, familiar voice.

"Hey," A voice boomed from inside the handball courts. "Look who it is, guys. Mitch the Bitch."

"Come on, Bobby," Mitch said, stopping just as he was about to hit the safety of the curb. "I've gotta get to class."

"Oh yeah? You hear that, guys? *Bitch* boy wants to get to class," Bobby said. He held a basketball in his hands, smacking it hard with his open right palm as he spoke.

"What a fucking *dork!*" Andre said with a laugh.

"Yeah, such a dork, man," Eric continued.

Andre and Eric were Bobby's *new* close friends. Also, a year older than Mitch, he'd had run-ins with them often throughout his freshman year. Like

Bobby, they were much bigger than Mitch, though, whereas Bobby was athletic, these two looked like they were on their way to becoming overweight adults. This didn't change the fact that Mitch knew they could smash him with little effort whenever they wanted.

"Look you guys. Why are you always messing with me? Can I just go to class in peace for once?"

"You got any money on you?" Bobby asked, smacking the basketball again. "Empty your pockets."

"Fine," Mitch said with a shake of the head, pulling the pockets from his jeans. The soft cloth hung down his legs, showing their emptiness. "You see? You happy now? Can I go?"

"No, not those pockets," Bobby said. His voice grew stern and fierce. "Your backpack pockets."

"Come on, Bobby," Mitch pleaded.

"Do it, bitch boy."

Mitch rolled his eyes, letting out the deepest sigh of his life. That act alone on the wrong day could warrant a fist to the guts or a freshly packed knuckle sandwich. But with the promise of cash, Bobby seemed to let these moves slide. He dropped his backpack to the ground, shuffling through the smallest pocket. From within, Mitch removed a 5 dollar bill and two singles. He held the crumpled bills towards Bobby, who quickly snatched them from his fingers.

"That's it? 7 bucks? Mitch the bitch. You know it costs more than that to pass."

"Well, that's all I've got today," He said, returning the backpack to his shoulders. "Sorry."

"I dunno, guys," Bobby said, looking back and forth at his two, massive followers. "Should we let him go this time?"

"Yeah, might as well," Andre said, his right hand on Bobby's shoulder. "But, remember. Next time, we might not be so friendly."

Mitch shook his head, refusing to give them any more acknowledgement. So much for some needed caffeine before class. Now he'd have to raw dog the entire day, fighting the heavy shades that continued to crash over his eyes. That was all the cash he had. So be it, he figured. At that moment, he didn't care about Bobby, his cronies, English or Math class. He only had one thing on his mind, and he wanted the day to be over so he could get back to the train tracks. The anticipation was eating away at him, hoping he just might run into the drifter again. He figured it to be a longshot, but against everything else in his life, this filled him with hope. As he walked away from the unpleasant interaction, something big hit him from behind. His head lurched forward, forcing him to stretch his arms in front of his body to brace a fall. He stumbled a bit, going to his knees. Bouncing next to him was the basketball Bobby had held. It had connected with the back of his head–*hard*. Direct hit. When he stood, he turned to the 3 boys as they laughed, his right hand rubbing the back of his head.

"Mitch the bitch," Bobby taunted. "What the fuck are you looking at, bitch boy? I told you to get to class."

"Fuck you, Bobby," Mitch barked. He immediately regretted this decision, but it had just slipped out. A reaction from a child who'd had too much. Words he couldn't take back, no matter how hard he pleaded.

"What the fuck did you just say to me, bitch boy?"

"I'm sorry–"

"We were going to let it slide today, too," Bobby said as Andre and Eric approached him. "But now, you're gonna get it, bitch."

Andre and Eric grabbed Mitch from either shoulder, escorting him towards the handball courts. He sauntered along with them, his feet almost dragging as they moved. They ushered him into the first stall of the courts, shoving him behind the wall. The three boys marched towards him slowly, Bobby pounding his fist into his open palm as Mitch stepped backwards, attempting to put distance between himself and them. When he hit the handball court wall, he looked side to side, wondering if he could somehow get away, though he knew deep down, this would not end well.

"We're gonna teach you a lesson you'll never forget, you little bitch boy," Bobby said.

He cocked back his right arm, thrusting it forward and burying it into Mitch's stomach. Bending forward, his body jerked from the blast as he fought to catch his breath.

"Let's try something new today, boys," Bobby said, a smirk growing on his angry face. "You still have that duct tape in your backpack, Andre?"

***

When the bell rang, it alerted the entire student body that the first period of the school day was well underway. It wasn't long before loads of freshman boys and girls came pouring from inside the gym for first period PE. For whatever reason, the school booked masses of freshman students for PE during the morning periods, scattering different coaches and assistants to chaperone and watch as the kids played different games and activities. Directly in front of the handball courts was a blacktop with numbers painted as far as the eye could see. Students, as they emerged dressed in their PE uniforms, were to stand on their assigned number and await further instructions for the day's activity. When the hundreds of students took their numbers, a smattering of laughter broke out amongst the crowd. It grew and grew until all the students pointed and laughed at the handball courts. One coach began blowing their whistle, trying to quiet the students.

"Hey, hey! Everyone knock it off!" He shouted. He leaned to another coach to his right. "What the hell is so funny?"

"Oh my god," The other coach gasped, her hand to her gaping mouth. "Turn around, look."

Behind them, stuck to the handball court wall with duct tape was Mitch. His body, covered from shoulder to ankle in the silver, sticky tape held him captive against the concrete wall, another strand pulled over his mouth. They had pulled his jeans down to his ankles, showing off his underwear to the entire class. There he stood, his eyes closed, as tears welled inside. The coaches rushed to him and began pulling all the tape from his body as his classmates continued their raucous laughter. Right then, he wished the drifter would appear before him and stick a knife into his chest and end his misery.

CHAPTER 5

For the next two weeks, Mitch had rushed home from school, dropping his backpack in his family's kitchen, wasting no time in darting to the train tracks. He would sit in one of the train cars pretending to flip through his magazine collection, throwing rocks or breaking glass bottles when he was lucky enough to find some. Looking for any way to pass the time hoping to run into the drifter yet again. He thought that maybe the excitement would wane as time passed by, losing interest in what he'd witnessed. But, somehow, his interest grew stronger by the day, almost by the hour. Every day as he rode his bike through the dirt towards those abandoned trains, he kept his fingers crossed that maybe that would be the day he'd run across another killing in progress. So much time had passed since that fateful Memorial Day, with no interest in anything but encountering the drifter again. His homework suffered, he lost touch with the few friends he had and his chores around the house piled up. Because of this, it was growing more and more difficult to leave each day after school. His father, Mr. Graves wasn't too pleased with the current state of Mitch's bedroom or the fact he'd had to drag the trash cans to the curb the past two weeks. And after a recent outburst from his father, it was clear he wouldn't allow his son to get away with skipping those duties much longer.

Attempting to rid his mind of the inevitable tongue lashing to come at home, Mitch sat on the edge of the red train car, his legs dangling towards the dirt and weeds. He flicked through one of the many magazines completely disinterested as the sun dipped behind the hills in the far distance. When it became too dark to see the curves in the women in his magazines, and knowing his parents would come looking for him soon, he returned the crate to its hiding place, jumping to the dirt, lifting his bike. From off in the distance, Mitch saw headlights approaching the abandoned containers, moving particularly slow. He bent, trying to get a good eye on the car that was headed his way, before sliding his bike underneath the train. He then jumped into the opening, hiding in the shadows of night, peering around the wall to monitor who it was and what they might be doing.

The car came to a full stop, its engine and lights shutting down, just outside the black train car. Mitch, his little fingers twisting around the opening, kept his eyes locked on the vehicle. The car was old, run down and sputtering and coughing its way through the field. The body looked as though it had more rust than original paint, its tires no longer matching. From the driver's seat, a thin, frail looking man exited and walked to the front bumper. His torn jeans and filthy white t-shirt painted a picture of another drifter who had found his way to the abandoned tracks. This wasn't all too surprising or new to Mitch. He and his pals had kicked away different drug paraphernalia they'd found scattered about in prior visits. And the empty beer bottles left behind in the dirt made for some entertaining afternoons, watching the glass explode and fly when chucked at a rock. Mitch just about laughed out loud in glee when he saw the familiar drifter step out from the passenger side. Similar torn rags covered his thin body, just like when Mitch had left him weeks before.

"So, where the fuck is this stuff, man?" The stranger asked, his hands out from his hips. "You have me drive you out to nowhere. You better have the shit you promised, man."

"Don't worry about it," The drifter said, his hands in front of his body, as though he was preparing to block an attack from the stranger. "I told you it's here, so, *it's here.* Alright? Follow me, I have it hidden in the train."

"What is it doing out here? You leave your stash in this old ass train? What if some kid comes across it?"

"It hasn't happened yet," The drifter said with a deep breath, pressing his hands into the cold, dusty steel, hoisting himself inside. "Besides, if I caught a kid out here fucking with my stuff, I'd put them through hell. Believe me."

The drifter extended his right hand to the stranger, pulling him into the container. Mitch could hear both of their footsteps as they moved about within. Their voices, muffled by the metal between the cars, still rang loud enough for Mitch to understand what they were saying to one another.

"Drugs," Mitch whispered to himself, his ear pressed to the wall, listening intently.

"Alright, so, where is it, man?" The stranger asked, stomping back and forth in the pitch black darkness of night. His tone sounded much less patient than before.

"Here, come over here," He heard the drifter say. "I've got it stashed in a box behind this crate. I just need your help to move the damn thing."

Mitch heard footsteps cross from one end to the other. Then, it sounded as though all hell broke loose in there. Feet crunched on the steel, squealing and squeaking as they dragged across the dirt and filth, almost like nails on a chalkboard, repeatedly. Mitch's eyes shot wide open, partially in fear, partially in pure excitement. He knew what must be happening just on the other side of those walls. The two men grunted at one another, spitting curse words and threats that flew freely through the air. Then a loud *CLUNK* noise bounced off the rusted metal, which Mitch assumed were the two falling over one another. The fighting sounded intense to Mitch, as bangs and curses continued to fill his ears.

"No, NO!" The stranger screamed, pleading for the drifter to stop. "Please, come on, man! Just take the case! I don't give a *fuck!*"

"I don't give a shit about that case!" The drifter screamed. "I only care about *this.*"

Mitch heard what he assumed was the knife puncturing the stranger. A subtle tearing sound, followed by loud gurgles, like air passing through a pool of water. Repeatedly, that slashing sound fluttered through the cool air. When he heard footsteps move across the container, he slowly stepped closer to the opening. Quietly, he lowered himself to the dirt, peering any way he could into the pure blackness where the drifter remained. Footsteps approached from within, as the drifter emerged from the shadows into pure view. His chest, face, hands and arms coated in crimson, a buck knife resting in his right hand. He took a big leap, landing beside Mitch.

"*You!?*" The drifter shouted, reaching for Mitch's collar. "What the *fuck* do you think you're doing here, huh?"

Mitch trembled as the drifter pushed his small body against the wall of the train. He held the knife to the boy's side, his teeth gritting as though he could strike him any second.

"I-I," Mitch stuttered, hoping to say the right words. "I came back. To find *you*."

"Why did you want to find me, huh? Did you tell anyone about me? Where are they? The cops hiding out there somewhere?"

"No! No, of course not," Mitch tried assuring him, his hands in front of his chest. "I want to *learn* from you."

"Learn? Learn *what,* exactly?" The drifter's eyes floated all over the landscape, looking for anything that might pop out of the darkness and come for him.

"I want to learn how to do, you know, what you do."

"*What I do*?" The drifter laughed deep. "What are you? Some psycho, kid? Just go home, alright? Forget what you saw and what you heard. Just go home and play with your toys, alright? Forget about me."

The drifter let go of Mitch's collar, returning his knife to a holster on his hip. He turned and walked towards the back of the rundown vehicle.

"Come on," Mitch pleaded, following him. "Show me the ropes. I can do it. I've got what it takes."

"Get the hell outta here, kid," He replied with a long roll of the eyes. He sunk a key into the trunk of the car, pulling the hatch open. "Don't you want to grow up and be a firefighter or something? A pilot, maybe? I don't know, follow in your old man's footsteps. Do whatever the hell he does? Why do you want to be a killer?"

"I don't want to do what my dad does," Mitch said, seemingly grossed out.

"Why, what does your old man do?"

"He's a pharmacist. You know that shop over on Grand Avenue, Graves Pharmacy? That's his shop. He owns it."

"No shit?" The drifter asked, intrigue filling his blood stream. He nodded his head, pulling a suitcase from the trunk. "Seems like a good way to make a living to me, kid. Now, scram."

Carrying the suitcase, he hurried back to the train. He laid the suitcase in the dirt, dropping to one knee beside it. He flicked the locks on the front, lifting the lid open to admire what was inside. When Mitch tried to get eyes on the contents, the drifter quickly slammed the lid shut.

"I can help you, and *while* I help you, you can teach me how to do it."

"I don't need your help, kid."

"Come on!" He pressed on. His body jumped with excitement.

"How do you plan to help me, exactly? Huh? You don't think I can handle this kind of business on my own? I've been doing shit like this since before you were born."

"I don't know," Mitch said, his eyes moving across the landscape, hoping to find the right answer floating somewhere in the darkness. "I could, like, clean up afterwards. Help you get rid of evidence? Be an alibi if you ever need it?"

"An alibi, huh?" He asked, licking the inside of his bottom lip.

"Yeah! Exactly!"

The drifter paused, letting out a sigh so deep it came from his thighs. He turned to Mitch, "You really wanna learn how to kill another human being, kid?"

"Yeah, I do," Mitch said in a whisper. "I've never really been interested in, well, *anything*. But, after I met you. After I saw that guy you killed, this is all I think about. I *know* I can handle it. I want to know how it feels. I want to feel someone's life slip between my fingers," His eyes transformed inside his skull, almost as though they were on fire. He held his hands in front of his face, staring at his twitching little fingers.

"Kid, I've got to be honest. You're actually kind of freaking *me* out," He kept his gaze away from Mitch, nodding his head as though he needed to rattle the thoughts within his brain to process them. He then returned to Mitch, staring deep into his eyes. "You're really serious about this?"

"Absolutely," Mitch said, as serious as he'd ever said anything.

"So, you say your old man's a *Pharmacist*, huh? Probably has a good chunk of change set aside," He whispered to himself, deep in contemplation. "You know, maybe we *can* work something out. Alright, here's the deal. You follow my instructions precisely, or you fuck off, you got that?"

"Agreed."

"You've got a change of clothes with you?"

"No," Mitch looked himself up and down.

"Then today, you watch," The drifter said, shuffling through the suitcase. "I can't have you going home drenched head to toe in blood. That'll raise *way* too many questions with your folks. But next time, bring a change of clothes, you hear me?"

"So there *will* be a next time?"

"Yeah," The drifter said with a smile, rubbing his chin as though he had a plan. "I think we can work something out."

CHAPTER 6

Mitch sat with his back against the cold steel, keeping a safe distance from the drifter as he went to work. Today, the drifter had told him, making sure he fully understood before proceeding, that he was to *watch* and learn, not *touch* and learn. The whole, look with your eyes not your hands, mentality. So, Mitch watched. He watched every move the drifter made with the dead body in that container. When Mitch had first climbed in, he stopped to glance at the man. Bone deep slash marks decorated the man's neck, thick puncture marks oozing quickly drying ichor across his chest. The man's eyes had dried as they remained open in the cooling, early summer air. Mitch quickly noticed that dead folks' faces didn't look real after the deed was done. They resembled something more like a weird art project interpretation of what a person should look like. Not just lifeless, it's as though their souls literally dissipated into thin air as they expired. They seemed hollow, empty. And, to Mitch, there was little to fear from them.

Now, it was time for today's lesson–dismemberment.

He watched from afar as the drifter hacked away at the dead man's joints. Chopping through the flesh and bone, discarding the remnants into thick, black bags. Similar to the ones he was familiar with when he had to rake the yard 3 times a week during the fall. He could work with those. They were familiar to him. Not everything was easy as it first seemed, as he found the sounds quite disturbing, as the steel blade crushed and cracked against bones and ligaments inside the lifeless body. An acquired taste, maybe, he figured. Or, another damn chore to go along with life. Hey, no one likes chores, right?

When the man had been reduced to nothing more than scraps, the drifter loaded multiple black bags into the trunk of the old vehicle. Once the man was stuffed inside, he slammed the trunk shut and wiped his hands clean in the open air.

"There you go, kid," He said, rubbing his palms together. "Lesson one, complete."

"So, what do we do now?"

"*We* do nothing," The drifter barked, moving back towards the suitcase resting in the dirt. "*I* will take the body and dispose of it."

"Where do you do that?"

"You can't just take a body to a dumpster behind the mini mart, OK?" He asked, kneeling again at the case. "You need to find a place that's safe. A place that isn't heavily trafficked. Not like a park or anything like that, unless you want the body to be found. Like, to send a message, maybe."

"What do you mean, a message?"

"Geez, kid. I didn't think there would be this many fucking questions when I agreed to this."

"Well, I don't know anything yet. How am I supposed to learn if I don't ask questions?"

"A message. I mean," He looked to the sky, hoping for the right answers to fall from the stars and land on his tongue. "Like, you ever seen a mafia movie? Like a hitman? A hitman might want the dead guy's friends to *know* he's dead. To scare them. Get it? A message."

"So, this was not a message?"

"No," The drifter laughed, pulling a rolled up wad of cash from the suitcase. "Absolutely not."

"Wait, this was all for money?" Mitch asked. He seemed perturbed by the revelation.

"Not exactly," He said with slight concern in his voice. "This is just a bonus."

Mitch turned from the drifter, taking a few steps back towards the vehicle. He held his chin, nodding his head, allowing his thoughts to fall into the correct places. He turned back to him.

"So, why do you kill, exactly?"

The drifter went still, not moving for some time. He dropped the wad of cash back into the suitcase, returning the locks to their original position. Grabbing it by the handle, he stood.

"Let's just say it's an impulse. Something I *have* to do. I have these," He sucked air through his teeth. "These urges. And when these urges hit me, I just *want* to kill. I don't expect that to make sense to you. Although, this weird fucking intrigue you have with killing, I'd imagine you're well on your way to understanding."

"So, you're a serial killer?"

"Sure," He said, walking past Mitch to the car. He opened the back, driver door, tossing in the suitcase. "You can say that. Why not? It has a certain, bad ass flair to it, doesn't it? But, all you really need to know is this guy, as well as the one before. They were bad dudes who had things that belonged to me. Things that I wanted. And what they got, they deserved. What I got in return, well, I feel like I deserved."

He slammed the back door shut, stopping at the front driver door. Letting out a deep sigh, he looked Mitch directly into the eyes.

"You really want to work together on shit like this, kid? You sure about this?"

"Yes, absolutely," Mitch said, excitement in his young voice. "When can we start the next lesson?"

"Whoa, slow down, Tiger. There's a strategy involved in things like this. We need to wait it out, find the right time and the right person."

"How will we know when everything is right?"

The drifter stared into the distance, remaining silent. He was lost in his thoughts, thinking through all the possibilities in front of him. Without saying a word, he opened the driver door, standing with his forearms resting on the window.

"Come back in exactly two weeks. You hear me? Two weeks. Meet me when the sun just falls, right at the golden hour. When we meet, I will have further instructions for you."

Mitch sat on his bike, watching as the car left the field with the drifter and the dismembered body of the bad man. When the taillights were fully out of sight, he peddled home. The night had long taken over the sky, and the only thing he knew for certain was that his parents would not be too happy with him coming home so late.

CHAPTER 7

Mitch kept his distance from the train tracks for those two weeks, just as instructed. Even when Mr. Looney got caught—again—with adult magazines, and Mitch found a fresh stack in the recycling bin one morning, he left them behind to be taken by the garbage truck. Those pristine, barely flicked through pages, gone forever to be torn to shreds and recycled into something new. Who knows? Maybe they would return to the same form, only to have similar content printed on them. Mitch could hope. Sometimes in those two weeks he found himself at the end of the cul-de-sac, staring out at the field, wondering what might be occurring out there. Those two weeks felt like an eternity, but it did Mitch some good all the same. He caught up on his homework and kept up on his chores. For two weeks, Mitch was the picture perfect son and student. His parents didn't know where this newfound eagerness had come from, but they didn't care, either. He even made the time to take care of his baby sister, Myrna, when they wanted to have a date night at their favorite Mexican restaurant for fish tacos. After everything, deep down, he was a good kid. A good kid, with a nasty secret.

The night before he was to meet the drifter back at the train tracks, Mitch couldn't sleep. All of that excitement from the first day poured over him like an avalanche. It kept him warm that night. He knew he needed to be tough, to remain brave and not chicken shit out. He had asked for this. So when the time came, he'd better show up.

After school that afternoon, it was back to business as usual. Mitch, as usual. He skipped his homework, deciding to handle minimal chores, or enough to keep his parents off his back. And as the day turned to dusk, he was on his bike, peddling like there was gold in that field for the taking. When he arrived at the tracks, he slid his bike under the red container, choosing to sit on the ledge, allowing his feet to dangle to the dirt below. This time, as instructed he'd brought a backpack full of extra clothes. The clothes he wore to meet the drifter were some of his yard work clothes. Jeans, t-shirt and a ratty hoodie that were meant for laborious tasks. Old junk he'd be fine living without, if it came to that. There, he sat and waited, hoping that the drifter would follow through with what he'd promised. Though, right then, Mitch gave him a 50/50 chance. In the end, all Mitch really knew about this man was that he was a drifter. Hell, he didn't even know the guy's name. He really had no reason to believe he would follow through or show his face ever again. But, to Mitch's pleasant surprise, after a long wait, the drifter appeared, jumping into the opening of the container behind Mitch, scaring the daylights out of him.

"You made it," The drifter said, his feet slamming into the metal flooring. He stood, crossing the railcar, taking a seat next to the boy.

"My god," Mitch said, his hand on his chest. "You scared the hell out of me."

"Shake those nerves off, kid," He said, patting the boys back. "I can't have you scared already. Nothing has happened yet. You ready for your next lesson?"

"Sure. I mean, I think so," He said, not making eye contact. "What's the plan, exactly?"

"I've been scoping the target for a while now," The drifter said, shuffling his position. "Every week, right about this time, I've seen our target outside watering his plants."

"Wait," Mitch said, shaking his head. "This is someone who lives in the neighborhood? Are you *crazy*?"

"Not your neighborhood. The one across the field, way back there," He pointed out the back door of the container.

Way in the distance was another community not so different from where Mitch and his family lived. Rows and rows of ranch-style homes stretched deep, with different side roads connecting them together. Mitch never went to that neighborhood, that side of the tracks. When he was younger, he wasn't allowed to travel that far from home. Now, at his age, the train tracks were as far as he was compelled to ride. He was relieved to know this target wasn't a parent from his own street. Taking the life of someone he knew might have been too much, he thought. He didn't feel ready for the advanced course just yet.

"So, who is it then?" Mitch asked.

"Don't worry about his name, that's for me to know. What you're going to do is lure him out here. Understand?"

"What? Like I'm some sort of bait?"

"Not exactly," The drifter muttered. "Look, you wanted to learn from me, right? If you want to learn, you need to listen more and talking way fucking less."

"Sorry," He said under his breath. "OK, lure the target. Got it. How will I do that?"

"Like I said," The drifter let out a sigh, already losing patience dealing with a young kid. "I've been scoping him out for a while now. His wife leaves to take their kid to, I don't know, it doesn't matter. Karate or some shit. When she leaves, he's alone. They don't eat dinner until she returns, which is usually about two hours from now. That gives us plenty of time to take care of business out here, and for me to handle what I need to after the fact."

"What do you mean, after the fact?"

"The fuck did I say about all the questions, kid?"

"Right," He shook his head, disappointed in himself.

Mitch's head spun with all the details. All this planning was much more than he ever realized it could be. He felt stupid, thinking this would be an easier process. He hadn't considered all the planning and prep work that would go into taking a man's life. But now, he was ankle deep. He was locked in, whether or not he liked it.

"I've been watching the neighborhood for the last two weeks. At this time of night, most families on that street are inside. Eating dinner, watching the news, who gives a shit what they're doing? It's perfect timing to get him to follow you out here, and then we can get started."

"How did you choose this specific guy, though?"

"He's a bad man, kid," The drifter said, his voice as stern and serious as it had ever been when talking to Mitch. "He deserves everything that is coming for him. Believe me. He's made his bed, and tonight, he's gonna lay in it."

The drifter stood, walking back to the opposite opening of the train car. He rested his hand against the cooling metal wall, gazing at the neighborhood way in the distance. Mitch soon followed, standing next to him.

"How do I lure him here?" Mitch asked, nervous to break the silence.

"You're a kid," The drifter said with a laugh. "I'm sure you'll think of something."

They stood together, discussing the plan at great lengths. Mitch was to run into the neighborhood–all while making sure not to cause a scene–and get the man to follow him to the train tracks. Once they arrived together, Mitch needed to get him inside the container, where the drifter would wait in the shadows, ready to pounce. It all seemed easy enough. Though, if so, why was Mitch so nervous? It wasn't the type of nervousness he'd expected, like when you're in the waiting room before a root canal. It was more like the excitement that came from the day before your birthday. When you were all but certain you saw your dad walk into the house with a box that looked eerily like the shape of a PlayStation. Anxiety aside, to his surprise, Mitch felt ready.

He took off through the field towards the neighborhood. To get onto the street, Mitch needed to climb through a cut in a chain-link fence, but that was the easy part. Walking slowly at first, he hoped he wouldn't alarm anyone or bring too much attention to himself. The neighborhood was all so similar to his own. One-story ranch homes, front yards with different trees growing in the lawns and well-manicured hedges lining driveways. Mitch noticed even the garage doors looked similar. They even had the same green electrical boxes placed just off the curb in the grass. As he paced the sidewalk, he tried his best to play it cool knowing their target was only a few houses up and on the left. When he stopped near a standup, community mailbox, he saw the man step out from the garage onto his driveway. He was a husky man, wearing short, dark blue shorts and a white t-shirt. His curly, black hair looked like a mess on top of his head, as he pulled on a garden hose to reach a flower bed at the side of his home. Mitch took off in a full sprint, stopping just in front of the mystery man.

"Mister, Mister!" Mitch shouted, bending over with his palms on his thighs. "I need your help!"

"Whoa, whoa," The man said, letting go of the trigger on the end of his hose, stopping the water. "What seems to be the problem, son?"

"It's my dog!" Mitch shouted. "He ran into the field and I can't get him back. Can you please help me look for him?"

"Where are your parents, son?" The man asked, his face squinched, looking around the neighborhood.

"They're not home!" Mitch barked. "They told me it was my turn to walk him and I dropped the leash. He busted through the hole in the fence. Please, Mister. Help me get him back!"

"OK, ok Son," The man finally agreed. "Come with me. I'll help you find your dog. You shouldn't be out in the field all alone. I've seen some weirdos hanging out there."

CHAPTER 8

Mitch raced through the dirt and weeds, the man—their target—following closely behind. He was proud of himself, not only for getting the man to follow him, but the way he zig-zagged through the field, looking every which way as he ran. He really felt like he sold the entire thing.

"Here doggy!" Mitch shouted, whistling as he went. "Here doggy doggy!"

"Son, what's the dog's *actual* name? I think he'd come to his name more than *doggy*."

Uh oh, he was caught off guard. *Think quick, Mitch*, he thought to himself.

"His name?" Mitch asked, stopping in his tracks. He looked at the man over his shoulder, "His name is Cocoa. He's a big, brown dog."

"Got it," The man said, buying the lie hook line and sinker. "Cocoa! Come on Cocoa! Time to come home, boy!"

Mitch thought of the first thing that came to mind, and it had worked. Luckily, the first thing that popped into his head was what cereal he'd had for breakfast. Probably wouldn't have gone over as well if he'd blurted out his last period class that day at school. No one would believe he had a dog named Biology.

"Come on, Cocoa!" Mitch screamed, his hands around his mouth. "Cocoa, *please!* Wait! I think I just saw him run under the train!"

Mitch took off like a bolt of lightning, and on cue, the man charged after him. When they reached the abandoned train cars, Mitch knelt next to the black container, peering underneath. The man, upon catching up to Mitch, took a couple deep breaths, planting his palms into his knees.

"Did you see him go under that thing?"

"Yeah, I think so, Mister," Mitch said, a sad whine in his voice. "Cocoa, come out buddy. Come on, Cocoa. Oh god, I'm a dead man."

"No, it'll be OK, son. We'll get him out. Mistakes happen. You're *not* a dead man," The man said, placing a hand on Mitch's right shoulder.

"No," A gravel filled voice said from above, echoing from the shadows within the container. "But *you* are."

A large piece of wood swung from the shadows, connecting directly with the man's forehead. He recoiled from the hit as warm, red liquid poured down his face, dripping through his fingers as he pressed his hands over the open wound. The drifter jumped from the container landing on the dirt, rising slowly, the piece of wood in his right hand.

"What the hell is this?" The man shouted, looking at his blood filled hands. "Who are you?"

"I'm the death you've dreamt about so many times," He whispered. "The reaper that haunts your nightmares."

He swung the board downward, crushing the man's left knee inwards, forcing him to fall to the dirt. He dug his hands in deep, curling his fingers in the dry, hard soil.

"Please," The man pleaded, one hand covering the wide gash on his face, the other held out towards the drifter. "Please, I have a wife and kids. I have *money!*"

"Oh, don't you worry," The nameless maniac whispered. "That'll be mine soon enough."

The drifter spun the piece of wood, stained with blood so deep, it was clear this board had been used in other attacks. Other murders. Dried stains of crimson that had since turned to black as it soaked deep into the pores and fibers of the lumber. He circled around the man, who now sat on his heels, pleading and crying for his life. He stood behind the beaten man, lifting the board high over his own head.

"Please, whoever you are. Let me go. I-I won't say a word. Just, please, let me go. I have a family."

"Don't we all," The drifter whispered, bringing the board down, crushing it into the back of the man's head.

He collapsed into himself like a bag of unfolded laundry, landing face first into the hard soil. Blood from two gashes spilled into the dirt, like old, discarded oil. The drifter dropped the board, moving quickly to lift the man. Reaching under his shoulders, he hoisted him upwards, the pure dead weight of him being almost too much to handle.

"Come on," The drifter grunted. "Grab his legs, help me get him inside."

"Is he dead?" Mitch asked, still kneeling by the container.

"No, just knocked out. He's got a pulse. Come on, already! *You* asked for this, so look alive and give me a hand!"

Mitch rose to his feet, looking around confused and nervous. He didn't know what to do with himself, his body seeming to stutter as he fought for the right words or actions to take.

"Come on, kid!" The drifter shouted, dragging the man the best he could.

Mitch jumped as though an electric pulse shot through his body from his feet. He grabbed the man by the ankles, lifting his legs to his waist. Together, they dragged the unconscious target to the entrance of the black rail car. The drifter knelt, wrapping his arms around his waist, hoisting him as high as his lack of muscle would allow. He heaved and heaved, positioning his body onto the open platform of dusty steel.

"Help me roll him inside," He grunted.

Mitch didn't respond. Instead, he followed as he was told. Grabbing the man from the waist and pushing with all his might until the body rolled into the container. They both knelt, their hands pressed into their thighs as they took deep, heavy breaths. Moving that much weight isn't easy, it can knock the breath out of stronger, more able-bodied men than these two.

"Are you having as much fun as you'd hoped?" The drifter asked, laughing through deep breaths.

"So, what do we do now?" Mitch asked, avoiding the condescending question at all costs.

"Well, normally he'd be dead by now. But, since you want this to be a learning process, we're going to be taking a different approach. Hop on inside, I'll show you everything."

CHAPTER 9

After a long wait, the man finally woke. Lifting his head, his chin resting on his chest, he blinked feverishly to allow his eyes to adjust to the darkness surrounding him. He stretched his neck, trying to relieve some of the deeply embedded pain pulsating through his joints and muscles. As his brain realized what position he was in, he rocked his body. Silver tape was pulled over his mouth and around the back of his head. His ankles were bound by the same sticky tape and his wrists behind his back. Muffled screams burst through the tape as he screamed for help to no avail. His eyes fixated on Mitch and the drifter as they emerged from the far corner of the container, approaching him from the darkness.

"Are you sure you're ready for this?" The drifter asked, his hands on his hips, almost judging Mitch.

"Of course," Mitch said, scoffing. "Just tell me what I have to do."

The buck knife hissed as the drifter dragged it from the sheath on his hip. He nodded toward their prisoner, Mitch following his lead. When the drifter knelt by his side, Mitch knelt along with him.

"I'm gonna show you where to stab someone so it ends quickly. You see," The drifter said, poking their prisoner in his right shoulder with the pointy tip of the knife. "If you sink it in *here*, it won't really be all *that* effective. It'll hurt like hell, trust me, but it'll merely piss someone off. Not going to be fatal."

The prisoner shook even more violently, realizing he was being reduced to nothing more than some sort of sickening murder dummy. An experiment. A prop in some weirdo murder 101 class. Muffled screams of *"What the fuck"* and *"Let me go"* drooled from behind the duct tape. His cries were useless, as the drifter and Mitch merely ignored his pleading for help.

"Now, you can always use a gun. But what you need to remember is that guns are loud. *Very* loud. And can be incredibly messy, although they finish someone off quickly."

"Is that why you use the knife?" Mitch asked, his eyes bright from the lesson.

"That's one reason," He replied, nodding his head. "I also prefer the work of a knife. I don't know, call it the artist in me."

He moved the knife, allowing it to hover over the left side of the man's chest.

"Now, this is where the heart is, OK? That's a good hit. A *very* good hit. Absolutely fatal. They may move for a little while after that strike, but not for long. That's like a headshot in one of those video games you probably play."

"Got it," Mitch said, nodding.

He held the knife against the man's throat, lengthwise, with the blade pressed against his flesh.

"Of course, there's always the throat. You stab someone in the throat directly, or, *my favorite*, a good, deep slash along the neck, fatal. No one can come back from that one."

"Oh, right," Mitch said, continuing to nod along. "That's what you did to uh, that one guy when I saw you, right?"

"I don't know, probably," The drifter shrugged. "I do that a lot. Hard to keep them all straight."

He continued, "Now, there's always the stab to the head. You know, go full zombie mode," He held the knife, pointy end down, towards the man's skull. "But then you're cracking through bone, too much work. You can also slash the inside of their thigh," He acted out slashing the upper part of the man's leg. "That'll make someone bleed out. It's really messy. If you want my advice, stick to the heart and the neck areas, OK?"

"Got it."

The drifter stood, taking in a deep, contemplating breath. When he let it out, he shook his head as a slight sigh escaped his mouth. He looked at the buck knife in his right hand, then looked at Mitch.

"Alright, little man," He said, handing the knife to Mitch. "Time for your test. Hope you ace it."

Mitch stood, reaching for the knife. He held it; the blade stretching over his right palm, the wooden handle held in his left hand. His mouth opened in awe as he gazed upon the shiny blade and rustic handle. Then, he looked at the drifter and nodded confidently without saying a word. The drifter, with a nod back in Mitch's direction, stepped aside to let the boy prove what he was worth. Show everything he'd learned in that short lesson.

Mitch took the handle in his right, squeezing his fingers around the dried, hard wood. He moved so that he stood directly in front of their prisoner, still shaking erratically, trying to break free and fight back in any way he could. As he screamed and sobbed, they were sure he was praying to be saved. Praying for someone to come along and see this sickening display and rescue him. But as the seconds ticked by, it was clear no help was on the way. This was his fate, as disturbing and as painful as it would be.

Mitch pressed the blade into the left side of the man's chest and pushed. It was much more difficult than Mitch had imagined, not considering having to slice through bone, tendons and everything else that stood between that blade and the meaty heart inside his chest. He gritted his teeth, pushing and pushing with every bit of strength he could muster.

"That's it, just like that," The drifter whispered, as though cheering him on. "Get it in there, really stab at him if you have to. Put some muscle into it."

Thick, red stains appeared under the white t-shirt, as the man stretched his head forward, his eyes locked in a painful, horrific gaze with Mitch's. His mouth open, muffled screams coming from behind the tape. Mitch adjusted his hands, pushing more and more as the knife slid through his flesh, popping through his chest until it sank to the handle. Mitch stood, leaving the knife sticking from their prisoner as he took a few deep breaths.

"Do you think I hit it?" Mitch asked, huffing.

"Looks like you got it pretty damn close, kid," The drifter said, kneeling to check the wound. To check the kids' work.

The blood spot on his shirt grew by the second as he writhed in pain, shaking and convulsing, banging his head against the steel wall.

"Go ahead, tear it out," The drifter instructed.

Mitch wrapped his hands around the handle, gritted his teeth, pulling the knife from the man's chest. Once the knife was torn from his flesh, the man's lifeblood erupted from the deep wound, shooting halfway across the train car, spraying Mitch as he backed away.

"Oh, baby!" The drifter shouted with a clap. "Yeah, you got him alright. I think we call that beginner's luck."

The man kicked his bound feet, lurching forward then slamming his body against the metal wall, resulting in loud clunking noises echoing from within the container. Worried someone might hear the commotion, the drifter pushed Mitch from behind.

"Come on, finish the job. Don't get scared now. This is *your* kill. Your *first* kill," He said, proudly nodding his head with a smile. He whispered, "Savor it."

Mitch knelt, pressing the blade against the man's throat and took a deep breath. He pulled his arm across the man's body in one swift motion; the blade slicing deep into his neck. As blood poured from the open gash, drenching his abdomen in warm crimson, he pressed the back of his head against the metal wall. Mitch remained knelt, his eyes locked into the victim's, admiring his life as it quickly slipped away. He watched as any sparkle in those eyes dimmed until they became hollow and lifeless, just like the man he'd seen killed weeks before. Soon, the cries and convulsing came to a stop, as the man's spirit left his body, leaving behind nothing more than a slashed shell of who he'd been in this life.

When they removed tape from his limbs, it was time for the second lesson of the day–dismemberment. Mitch had already received his lesson on this, so instead of talking much, they got right to it. The drifter had to assist in this task, Mitch being too young and weak to cut through some of the tougher areas of the human body. Together, they hacked at their prisoner, stuffing his parts and limbs into thick, black plastic bags. When all was said and done, they stuffed the now full bags underneath the train car before sitting on the edge of the steel container, both sets of legs dangling in the evening breeze. Their clothes no longer resemble anything close to what they had before. Splattered, stained and soaked in the man's body fluid.

"So, how'd I do?" Mitch asked, a look of pride on his face.

"I'd say you knocked it out of the park, kid. Good work. You're clearly a natural."

It tickled Mitch. So proud of himself.

"So, what do we do with him?"

"Don't worry about that," The drifter said, waving it off. "I'll take care of the disposal. Let's leave that for a more advanced class. I've got a car around the corner. I'll throw the bags in the trunk and get it done."

"What should we do next? What other bad guys are on your list? Wait, do you have a list?"

"No, I don't have a list," He let out a hearty laugh. "I'm not a vengeance fighter, kid. I act when I feel the need to act. Never need to have anything planned."

"When will I know to come find you? To do it again?"

"Well, I *did* have an idea," The drifter said, rubbing his chin in thought. "Do *you* know any bad guys who need dealing with?"

Mitch's head spun. He hadn't even considered the idea of killing someone he knew. The game just became way too real way too fast. Until now, he had only seen strangers dead or dismembered. No one he'd known personally. To this point, killing someone he knew wasn't something he'd even wanted to consider, and hoped it wouldn't even come up in conversation.

"Eh, I don't know."

"You asked for this. *You* wanted to learn. What did you expect? To keep dealing with strangers? Keep having me provide the examples for your amusement? Give me a break. Think, this is your chance to get even with someone you've always wanted to deal with. Someone you've always wanted to get back at."

His head continued spinning round and around. He knew he'd asked for this, but he wasn't sure if he was ready for things to hit so close to home.

Though, he was pretty certain that he couldn't back out now. He'd opened a box and was sure it would be impossible to stuff what he'd pulled out back in.

"Come on, kid," The drifter urged. "Whose insides do you want to see on the *outside*?"

Mitch thought for a moment, staring at the dirt, his mind spinning a million miles a minute.

"There is this bully," He whispered. "Bobby. At school. He picks on me and beats up on me. He's a real asshole."

"Alright then, Bobby it is."

"Wait, I'm not saying him for sure."

"Well, who else? Who else deserves to be taken care of? He's beating you up? Bullying you? Time to get even if you ask me. Sounds like my idea of a bad guy."

"You think so?"

"I *know* so."

"So, what? I bring him here and you help me, you know, *deal* with him?"

"No," The drifter shook his head, an evil smile on his face. "You lure him here, and then, *you* deal with him."

The drifter motioned his hand across his neck while making a *slash* sound. Mitch trembled at the idea, but he knew what he'd have to do. He needed to remember that he'd asked for this, and there was no backing out now.

CHAPTER 10

The following Friday, Mitch persuaded his 6th period teacher to release him early. It wasn't difficult—he demanded he needed to use the restroom, and, with it being so close to the end of day, he argued, what was the point in returning to class? Besides, Fridays aren't only coveted by students. Teachers want out of the classroom as soon as possible all the same. Not all teachers are working for the week, some are biding time until the weekend comes, just like the kids. Mitch waited for the bell to ring, his back against the wall in the main hallway that cut through the campus. He stood underneath the wide overhang that covered the hallway, anxiously tapping his foot. The moment the bell rang, students poured from classroom doors like a flood. Papers flew through the air, accompanied by countless conversations as students crashed into one another, headed down the hallway towards the entrance of the school. Mitch, remaining against the wall, peered the best he could over the steadily moving crowd, waiting to get eyes on someone. When he finally saw Bobby stomping through the hall, he pushed his body from the wall, shoving through the crowd to meet him.

"Bobby, wait up!"

Slowly turning, Bobby's hollow eyes jumped all around, looking for the ghostly voice calling from behind.

"What do you want, bitch boy?"

"Here," Mitch said, pulling a five-dollar bill from his jeans pocket. "I knew when you saw me, you'd ask about it. So, I figured I'd make it easy on you for a change."

"Hey, what do you know?" Bobby said, tucking the bill into his front pocket. "Mitch the bitch is finally learning. It's good to see your progress, dude."

Bobby quickly turned to continue the trek towards the parking lot, not wanting to waste another second within the confines of his high school before his weekend.

"Bobby, wait," Mitch called from behind. "I-I wanted to ask you something."

"What is it, bitch?"

"So, like," Mitch stuttered. His nerves showing on his sleeve. "What are you, uh, what do you have going on this weekend?"

"Why?" Bobby's face squinched in confusion.

"I was kind of wondering if you wanted to maybe, I don't know, hang out? Like old times?"

"Why would I want to do that?"

"I don't know," Mitch's voice fell to a low mumble. "We could hang out at the old train tracks. You know, in that field out by my house?"

"Yeah, I remember," Bobby said, scratching the back of his head. "I remember we used to break bottles out there and shit."

"Yeah, totally! Say," Mitch leaned in, lowering his voice. "In one train, you'll never believe it. I stole a bunch of nudie mags from my neighbor. I'm talking, like, an entire library of them."

"No shit?" Bobby's ears perked up.

"You want to meet up out there? We can break shit, look at some nudie mags. You know, just hang out. Like old times."

After pondering the suggestion for a moment, Bobby finally spoke. "Can you get any beer?"

"Beer?" Mitch considered the question. "I could probably lift some from my dad. He always has my mom buy it from the Price Club, and it just sits in the back of the fridge."

Bobby nodded at the idea of spending a Saturday with Mitch, wondering if it was worth his time.

"You know what? Why not? I could be down for some beers, hot chicks and breaking shit. When are you going to head out there?"

"How about tomorrow? Just before sunset? I'll meet you there by the old train tracks and we can just, you know, *hang*."

"Alright," He said, a smile growing on his face. "I'll see you there. But, don't forget the beers."

"Cool, dude. I won't," Mitch said, lifting his hand as though he expected a high-five.

Bobby reluctantly obliged, awkwardly connecting his palm with Mitch's.

"And Bobby. Don't tell anyone else about the stash of magazines. I don't want a bunch of people to know I've got them hidden out there."

"Don't worry about it, dude," He said, turning to walk away. A sly smile washed over his face. "Your perverted secret is safe with me."

CHAPTER 11

Mitch arrived early to the tracks. Before he'd left home, he had filled a backpack with cans of beer that had found their way to the back of the family fridge. It seemed that his parents had forgotten the older beers, now pushed well behind containers of leftovers, fresh groceries and baby formula. He was confident his parents would never notice them missing, as those cans always had a way of building up and taking up space before being thrown away to be replaced with fresh ones. He didn't understand why his dad asked his mother to buy them in the first place, allowing them to rot and go untouched. This evening, he didn't care. It served his purpose.

Skidding his bike in the dirt, he kicked up a large cloud of dust and dry dirt into the air. He dropped his BMX, climbing directly into the train car. Nervousness had overtaken him, as he shuffled back and forth, burning a path in the dusty, steel floor. Dropping his backpack and leaving it against the wall, he pulled the crate of adult magazines into clear view. It scraped and squealed across the dirty floor, as he took a seat, his back pressed into the cold metal. Opening the backpack, he retrieved a can of beer. For a second, he considered guzzling it down to kill his nerves, but promptly returned it to the bag. There he remained, stomping his feet and twiddling his fingers in nervous anticipation for Bobby to arrive. Did he really have it in him to pull this off? Did he even *want* to? Nothing he could answer yet, he figured that maybe he'd know in the moment. Startling him from his anxiety induced stupor, the drifter jumped through the opening at the back of the train, landing hard with an echoing boom. The loud smash of his boots against the metal floor nearly made Mitch's skeleton jump from his skin.

"Dude," Mitch said, catching his breath. "You scared the shit out of me. You could've killed me from a heart attack."

"Sorry about that," The drifter said with a deep laugh. "So, are you ready or what?"

"I think so."

"Look, kid," He whispered, shuffling in front of Mitch. "You've got to get your head straight. You make one mistake out here, and he could either get away and rat on your ass. Or, he could kill *you* instead. You want that to happen?"

"Of course not," Mitch scoffed, pushing his body into the wall to create distance.

"Then look alive, kid. Here, take this," The drifter extended his right hand. Inside, he held a brand new, shiny knife. The black handle had a strip of silver that cut from one end to the other. When he clicked a button on the side it released a spring loaded blade over 3 inches long. He nodded at Mitch, instructing him silently to take the knife.

"You got this? For me?" Mitch asked, surprised. His eyes were bright and flickering even in the shadows.

"I know it's not much. But, it's a good beginner blade. Besides, you shouldn't need one like mine, *yet*. It's too big for your hand size. Go ahead, hold it. See how you like it. Get used to the weight, how it moves, how you can swing it."

Mitch jumped to his feet, holding the knife in his open palm. While gripping the handle he swung it forward, pretending as though he was thrusting it into someone's guts. He then struck downward, before standing up straight and nodding with a smile.

"Feels perfect," He said, his voice filled with glee.

"Good," The drifter replied, standing to his feet. "I'm going to be right next door. Just in case you get yourself into any trouble. Besides, I'll have to help you dispose of this little shit when you're through."

The drifter jumped from the train landing hard into the packed dirt. In a flash, he disappeared into the second container out of sight. When Mitch stepped to the opening, he saw something he had feared since this plan took shape. Riding bikes towards the tracks was not only Bobby, but he had brought Andre along with him.

"Fuck," Mitch whispered, wiping sweat from his forehead.

He closed the blade, shoving the knife into the back pocket of his jeans. Chewing at his fingernails he began walking in a circle muttering curse words to himself. What should he do? What *could* he do? This wasn't part of the plan. *Two* classmates? No, this was too much. This wasn't the plan. Far from it. He quickly shifted his mindset figuring today really would be about stolen beer and nudie magazines and nothing more. He'd have to entertain his tormentors with free drinks until they decided it was time to go. As this reality struck his mind, he heard their bikes hit the ground.

"Mitch?" Bobby shouted. "Hey, Mitch? Where are you?"

Mitch slowly emerged from the shadows, bending around the opening. A scowl had taken over his face, clearly showing he wasn't all too happy with the uninvited guest now standing before him.

"Hey Bobby," Mitch muttered. "What's Andre doing here?"

"Hey, bitch boy!" Andre shouted, clapping his hands. "Heard you had some good *reading* material and some beers for us! I couldn't pass up the opportunity."

"Fine," He said, caving. He shook his head. "But maybe lay off the bitch boy stuff while we're together, huh? I'm the one providing everything here. Not you."

"What's with the unnecessary hostility, bro?" Andre asked, lifting himself into the container. Bobby followed closely behind. "We're just kidding around, man."

"It's cool," Bobby said, wrapping his arm around Mitch's shoulder. "Mitch is cool. Right, Mitch?"

"Sure," He muttered under his breath, staring at his feet.

"See? I told you he was cool. Now, get me a beer, buddy. I'm thirsty."

***

The three of them sat together in an awkward, open circle as they each flipped through different adult magazines. Andre and Bobby seemed elated with the library of content they could never view when at home–or anywhere else. A serious collection of oohs and aahs filled the air as they tilted some magazines to their sides, leaning in real close to catch every inch of the ladies in the photos. Mitch had stuffed 8 cans of beer into his backpack, thinking at first it might be overkill. But, not with Andre and Bobby now calling the shots. Now, he figured that wasn't enough with these two delinquents. They crushed through those cans with a quickness, Bobby chugging his last one down before crushing the empty can in his right hand, tossing it into the corner. He let out a deep belch that echoed off the steel walls.

"Hand me another beer, Mitch," Bobby said, his right hand extended.

"They're gone."

"Seriously? That blows."

"Did you even drink one, bitch–I mean, Mitch?" Andre asked.

"No. I didn't want one, but thanks."

"Well, they're gone, so I wasn't really offering. What, you don't drink beer? Dude, I thought Bobby said you were cool."

"I *am* cool," He shot back. "I just, I don't like the taste of beer."

"Pssht," Andre bursted out. "Who does?"

"Well," Mitch thought for a moment. "I-I like mixed drinks. You know, cocktails. Those are more my style."

"Yeah right," Andre said with a roll of the eyes. "Look, I've gotta take a piss. I'll be back."

Andre jumped from the container, dashing out of sight to relieve himself in the dirt. Mitch stood as well, pacing the floor yet again while Bobby remained sitting, his back against the wall.

"Don't mind Andre, dude," Bobby said, catching Mitch's attention. "He's cool and all, but he can be a real dumbass. He doesn't mean anything by it. Besides, he doesn't know how far back you and I go."

"How far *back* we go?" Mitch asked, shooting around. "Maybe it's because you torment me *daily* at school. Maybe that's why he's so mean to me."

"Nah," He scoffed at the idea. "I told you, we're just playing around, man. Relax."

A light thump came from just outside the train car. Mitch looked over his right shoulder at the wide opening, his eyes opened in fear. *Oh shit*, he thought to himself. *The plan must be underway.* Mitch hadn't told the drifter about the unanticipated guest, and that it would be best to abort the mission. It sounded as though the drifter took things into his own hands, moving things along swiftly.

"What the hell was that?" Bobby asked, motioning as though he might stand.

"No!" Mitch shouted before regaining his composure. "I mean. No, stay there. I'll take a look. It's probably just Andre screwing around."

"Yo, Andre!" Bobby shouted, settling back into his spot. "Wrap it up, would ya? It's gonna be dark soon. We need to take off."

Mitch approached the opening with caution, wrapping his fingers around the edge before peering into the open air. His eyes shot open as his mouth dropped when he saw what had created the thud they'd heard. There he saw Andre, his feet dangling inches above the dirt, a thick rope wrapped tightly around his neck. The hands of the drifter were all Mitch could see coming out from the darkness. Those thin, creepy, filthy fingers pulling the rope into the air, strangling Andre. Andre's face contorted as he fought to breathe, frantically clawing at the rope that strangled the life out of him. Two dust covered sneakers hung in the air, kicking back and forth, trying to connect with the ground. When his eyes turned to his left, he saw Mitch. He reached for his classmate, attempting to mouth something to him. As the breath and life drained from his young body, his flailing slowed, resembling a dead fish discarded in the sun on a wooden dock. As his body turned limp, the drifter let his body down slightly, when a hand shot from the shadows, thrusting a knife deep into Andre's chest. Then, the rope pulled back again, lifting his lifeless body up into the container to be eaten by the shadows.

Mitch turned back to Bobby, reaching behind him, pulling the knife from the back pocket of his jeans. He kept his hands hidden, as he clicked the blade open, taking small steps towards Bobby.

"You see him out there?"

Mitch didn't reply.

"Hey, Mitch," Bobby looked up from the magazine. "You see him out there or what? Andre!"

Still, Mitch said nothing. He stared at Bobby through the top of his eyes, taking small, calculated steps towards him.

"Mitch, what the fuck is wrong with you? What are you doing?"

When Mitch was within reach of his classmate, he pulled the knife from behind his back, shoving it deep into the right side of Bobby's chest. Terrified of what he'd done, quickly he pulled the knife from his skin, a stream of blood following the blade, splashing onto the floor.

"What the *fuck!*" Bobby shouted, pressing his left hand over the open, gushing wound. "You son of a bitch. I'm going to *kill you!*"

Without hesitation, Bobby was to his feet rushing towards Mitch. Mitch, his mouth hanging open in shock, took frantic steps backwards trying to get away from the charging bully. It was no use, as Bobby tackled Mitch like a defensive lineman pummeling a quarterback. Mitch landed hard on his back with Bobby sitting on top of him. Bobby wrapped his hands around Mitch's neck, squeezing tighter and tighter as the anger inside him built to a fever pitch.

"You stupid fuck," Bobby uttered through grit teeth. Spittle and saliva falling from his lips. "You're a fucking *dead man!*"

Bobby lifted his right hand into the air, closing into a fist. He struck downward with whatever strength he had, the pain in his right shoulder growing in intensity. When his fist connected with the left side of Mitch's face he let out a painful groan. Bobby again wrapped his hands around his neck, continuing to squeeze tighter and tighter.

The grunting from Bobby and gasping for breath from Mitch were both interrupted by a wet sound resembling a boot being pulled from the mud. A loud suck of air followed. Bobby's hands released from the boy's neck, his jaw falling and his eyes shooting open. When Mitch opened his eyes, he saw the drifter standing over them. He had thrust his buck knife deep into Bobby's side, cutting clear through his ribs, cartilage and everything else in its path, puncturing his right lung. The drifter turned the blade as it rested between two of his ribs, pulling back on it with an intense jerking motion, tearing the knife from his body.

Bobby fell off of Mitch, landing on his back. He writhed in pain, kicking his feet into the floor, both of his hands pressed against his ribcage.

"There," The drifter said, frustrated. "Now he's all yours. Get the job done and do it *right* this time."

Mitch tried pulling himself together, resting on the backs of his feet and rubbing his left eye. He reached for the knife that had fallen to the ground in the scuffle before standing to his feet. Standing over Bobby, he admired the bully as he wriggled in unimaginable pain. His chest, heaving as he gasped for air with his punctured lung.

"Please," He muttered, blood appearing within his mouth and dripping down his pale cheeks. "Don't kill me, *please*. I'm just a kid."

"You're a piece of shit bully," Mitch said, anger building in his body. "It's time you get what's coming to you."

Mitch sat on his chest, lifted the knife high into the air, furiously stabbing down connecting the blade with his flesh. Thrust after thrust, he pulverized his chest, neck and hands, as Bobby tried with every bit of his being to fight off the constant stabbing. When Mitch finally had enough, he screamed, his young voice bouncing off the walls of the train car. Lifting the knife high above his head, he plunged the blade straight through Bobby's neck. He tore the blade to the left, as it sliced everything in its path, freeing itself through the side of his throat. Bobby gurgled as he fought to breathe, his body covered in crimson from the many stab wounds that now decorated his body. Mitch sat on his chest, watching as the light in his eyes went dark. Taking a deep breath, Mitch stood.

"I thought you didn't kill kids," Mitch asked, turning to the drifter.

He remained quiet for a moment, admiring his protégé's work.

"I guess I do now," He finally said, sending a chill through Mitch's body.

CHAPTER 12

They spent the rest of that evening with a whole new type of lesson for young Mitch. A lesson he wasn't sure he was prepared for, though now, with what had transpired, it did not leave him with much of a choice. He now had to assist in not one, but two dismemberments, both of which for people he knew personally. Prior to this, the drifter had taken the helm regarding the disposal of his victims. Though, this day was all for Mitch. Bobby was meant to be *his* victim. The second teen tagging along turned out to be a victim of circumstance. An unfortunate addition to the night's activities. Now, with two bodies to be dealt with, the drifter clarified Mitch needed to get busy doing his part to clean up and dispose of the mess they'd made.

Together, they dragged and carried Andre's body into the container where Bobby's body remained, resting now in an eternal state of panic in a pool of his own congealing blood. Mitch watched closely as the drifter thrust a rusty machete at Andre's body–his shoulders, thighs, ankles and wrists, before focusing on the neck area. He watched as the man made it look easy, like it wasn't a chore even in the slightest hacking through the flesh and bone of his victim. Every few hacks, he looked at Mitch, a look of disgust and disappointment on his blood splattered face.

"Come on, kid," He grunted, swinging away at the left shoulder. "He's fucking dead, alright? He's not gonna do the work for ya. And don't think I'm going to take on the entire job." He slashed again at the lifeless body.

Mitch cringed as he tried to use his own machete, the blade rusted and decaying, to hack away at Bobby's right shoulder. He felt like he was in science class, when he was creeped out at the idea of having to use a scalpel and cut through the abdomen of a frog. It reminded him of the strong smell of the formaldehyde that tainted the room, and how it made his stomach turn. Now, it wasn't chemicals meant to preserve that turned his stomach; it was the ever growing metallic smell filling his senses, and the feel as Bobby's fluids caked and dried to his skin. Using the weakened blade to saw through the first layers of flesh was easy. But what remained underneath the skin made it damn near impossible to continue with his squeamish approach.

"Hey!" The drifter shouted, using the back of his arm to wipe the splatter from his face. "The kids already dead. You're not going to hurt him any worse than you already have. Hack at it. *Slash* away. That sawing shit might work on some weeds in your backyard, but that ain't gonna cut it here. Let me show you."

The drifter dropped his machete, walking across the container with an annoyed huff. He tore the object from Mitch's hands, grabbed Bobby by his cooling, right wrist, lifting his arm into the air.

"Put some strength into it, kid," He said, lifting the machete high into the air. "Like this."

Whack! Whack! Whack!

He swung the long blade through the air, landing a perfect hit each time into the top of his right arm. Mitch watched as the blade pulverized everything in its path, slicing through the tendons, muscles and bone that connected his arm to his body. When he was done, he held the disembodied arm as it softly dangled in the open, evening air.

"You see?" He asked, dropping the arm. It landed on the cold, steel flooring with a dull thud. He handed the machete back to the kid. "I told you, I'm not doing all the work this time. Now, get this done. I don't want to be here all fucking night."

Mitch didn't say a word. The only gesture he could muster was a soft nod in agreement. He lifted the machete above his head, both hands clasping the handle tight. With a few slashes downward, he connected the rusty blade into Bobby's left thigh until he felt he had cut through enough of the connective tissue to make the break. He grabbed the leg by the ankle, pulling with all his might. The tendons and tissues snapped and crackled in the quiet air until the leg pulled from the rest of his body.

"There you go," The drifter said, finally sounding slightly proud of his young protégé. "Now, do the rest. Just like that."

Again, Mitch could only nod in agreement. He wiped the sweat from his forehead, leaving streaks of dark red across his face as he stood, fighting to catch his breath. Following the same plan of attack, he pushed himself to the brink, slashing and hacking the body to pieces, saving the head for last. He held the handle with both hands and took a deep breath. *Whack! Whack! Whack!* The blade crashed into the neck until his head dipped back and rolled to the right. When the head settled, Bobby's wide open, terrified eyes were staring directly at him.

The drifter tossed a box of black garden trash bags inside the train car, instructing Mitch to fill them with the chopped body parts. They remained quiet during the process, helping one another carry the bags to the back of a nasty old van the drifter had driven. He'd left it in the adjoining neighborhood until the deed was done, hoping not to alert anyone of their activity. Rust and decay had overtaken the white paint that once graced the body, and Mitch noticed that none of the wheels matched. A real piece of junk, but it would get the evidence far away from the train and from Mitch.

"Where did you get this thing?" He asked, dropping a bag into the back. "You had a car with you last time."

"Don't worry about it," The drifter said through deep, heavy breaths. "I have many ways of doing things."

"You know, you never told me your name," Mitch said, walking side by side with the man back to the rest of the bags.

"It's better that way," He said. "We don't need to be that familiar. Besides, I enjoy a level of secrecy in what I do."

"Yeah, but, we sort of work together now. Shouldn't we have *some* familiarity with one another?"

"Look kid," He said, lifting a bag over his shoulder. "Let's not forget that you stumbled upon me and what I do. I took you in initially so you wouldn't rat me out. All this other shit, well, it helps me do what I do and get what I need to survive. One of these days I'll be on the move. And when that time comes, we don't need to be on the lookout for one another."

"I'd tell you my name," Mitch said, a slight sense of annoyance in his voice. "I don't care if you know my name."

"I don't want to know your name," He said. "It's not important to me."

They continued to fill the van without saying another word to each other. When the van was packed full and tight, the drifter slammed the doors, pushing his body weight into the right door, ensuring it snapped shut.

"I'll dispose of this shit for us," He said, looking at his hands and wiping them on his filthy pants.

"You don't want my help?"

"Nah, I can handle this. Besides, same as before, I don't want a random kid in the car if shit goes sideways, you know?"

The drifter pushed past Mitch, opening the driver door.

"But wait," Mitch called to him. "Do you have another target? Who's going to be next?"

The drifter stood quietly for a moment, staring at the dirt. He looked over his right shoulder at the kid with a strong, contemplative look.

"You're *really* ready to do this again?"

"I mean, yeah. So, do you have someone else in mind? Another target I can lure out here?"

"Now that you mention it, I *do* have a very specific target in mind," He said, his eyes squinted towards the young boy.

"Who is it this time?"

"Don't you worry about that. I'll get it all figured out. Just meet me out here next week, same day and time."

The drifter hopped into the van, slamming the door behind him. Mitch rushed to the door, speaking through the closed window.

"But how will I know the plan? How will I know what you need me to do?"

He rolled the window down before speaking.

"Just wait out here and the plan will fall into place," He said, turning the ignition. The old, shitty engine barked and coughed as it turned over.

"You'll know exactly when the plan is in motion. *Trust me*. This time, you won't be able to miss it."

As Mitch walked to his BMX, the drifter called to him.

"You bring the backpack, like I told you? Extra set of clothes and all?"

"Of course," He said.

"Change your clothes and clean yourself up before you head home. We don't need your parents asking questions about why you're soaked in body fluids and torn flesh remnants. I'll see you soon, kid. You won't be able to miss me. Trust me, kid."

CHAPTER 13

The following week wasn't only slow, it was also rather painful for young Mitch, as the entire city had erupted with anguish over the two missing teenage boys. Fear and anxiety had taken over the hearts and minds of parents and children alike after Bobby and Andre disappeared. The local police had assumed control of the high school, monitoring every movement the students made, questioning anyone and everyone they could think of that might have had anything to do with the boys and their sudden disappearance. It was well known around the school that the missing boys were bullies to younger students, which meant it was only a matter of time before they called in Mitch for questioning. He knew the time would come, and he felt prepared for the inevitable meeting. Though, his mental prep didn't make it any easier when the principal pulled the door to his English class open, motioning for Mitch to follow him and an escorting officer to the front office.

Nervousness poured from him like a flood, sweat building on his forehead, his palms buried deep into his jean pockets to soak up the liquid that had gathered. He spoke softly and kept his sentences short during the questioning. It was everything he had expected–*What do you know about the whereabouts of Bobby and Andre? Do you know where they hung out outside of school? Did you have any contact with the boys in the last week?* It was much easier to lie than Mitch had imagined. He could stick to the truth–his own truth–that the boys hated and tormented him any chance they got, and he made a point of staying away from them. He shared how he and Bobby were once friends, but since high school, it had been made perfectly clear that he was no longer welcome in that crowd, so he tried to keep his distance. Maybe it was the nerves, maybe it was the fear of being caught, but he even spilled a few tears during the exchange. Somehow he felt that helped his case, and he was proud of himself for doing so. When they told him he was free to go back to class, a wave of relief washed over him he'd never experienced before. To Mitch, it was a glorious feeling. He had completed his first *official* kill. One where he made the plans, he set the stakes. And until now he had gotten away with it. A massive smile wrapped his face as he wiped tears from his cheeks on his way back to English.

The third bully friend, Eric, was an absolute mess after their disappearance. Wandering about, almost zombie-like to and from class, alone. He wouldn't say a word to anyone, not even responding to other students if they addressed him. One day after class, Mitch noticed him sitting on the front steps of the school, staring at the concrete, tearing apart a small piece of paper.

"Hey Eric," Mitch said quietly, hoping not to force the volcano within him to erupt. "You doing OK?"

Eric's eyes remained staring at the concrete giving no sign of acknowledgement.

"Hey man, you know," Mitch said, pushing his right hand over the top of his head. "If you need anything, or just want to, I don't know, maybe talk sometime. You can always come to me."

"Why?" Eric asked, finally shifting his attention to Mitch.

"I can't imagine how you must be feeling. Your best friends missing and all. I don't know, I just thought maybe you could use a friend."

"When have you and I been *friends*?"

"We're not. I just," He looked away, fearing too much eye contact could lead to a punch in the nose. "I thought maybe you could use one right about now. I just wanted you to know that I'm around if you need anything."

Eric remained silent for a moment as Mitch's words bounced around within his skull. The three of them were never considered the sharpest tools in the murder kit, so Mitch wasn't the least bit surprised it took some time for him to fully grasp what he was saying.

"Thanks, dude," He finally said with a nod. "That's cool of you."

"Well, I guess I'll see you around, huh?"

"Hey, Mitch," Eric yelled as he walked away from him. "When they do turn up, don't tell them I've been all sad and shit, huh?"

"Why wouldn't you want your friends to know you were sad they were missing, Eric?"

"I don't know," He muttered, losing eye contact.

"You're not a bad guy, Eric," Mitch said with a friendly smile. "It's OK to care about your friends. They might even appreciate it."

"Yeah, maybe," He tossed a rock against the cement steps. "Just don't say anything, alright? I don't want them to call *me* a bitch, too."

"You got it, Eric," Mitch said through a deep sigh.

***

The night Mitch had waited for had finally come. It was time yet again to meet his nameless friend at the abandoned train cars for what Mitch imagined was another kill. He itched with excitement over who it could be this go around. Who could the bad man be? Or maybe this time he might be instructed to lure a woman to the kill site. He had only witnessed and taken part in killing men thus far, though that fact didn't bother Mitch. He knew it was usually men who deserved it. Still, he sparkled with the idea of who it could be. Maybe someone who had done the drifter wrong, like that drug dealer or even another killer? Maybe it was someone who treated their wife and kids like shit? Or, could it be a sex criminal? That would thrill Mitch. Scum like that deserved whatever street justice was awaiting them. And from what he'd seen, that drifter could deliver punishments that didn't enter most people's nightmares.

Mitch sat on the edge of one of the train cars, his little legs swinging in the open air. The sun continued to fall beyond the horizon; the night taking over quicker and quicker, yet the nameless killer never showed. As the darkness took over any remaining light, he shivered. Not just from the chill in the air, but also from being alone with the ghosts that now lived in and were stuck forever within those containers. His own hands had created some of those ghosts. As the memories from within those containers materialized, he felt a heaviness in the air. It made his skin crawl. He had now killed in that very spot, and he could almost feel lingering eyes peering upon and judging him from deep within the shadows. The longer he waited, the more scared he became. When the night had fully replaced the day, he decided maybe it was best to head home. He'd be back again in the following days, and he fully expected to see the drifter again. What did he know? Maybe something came up? Did he cross the wrong person, another killer who bested him? Ended his life before the drifter could deliver that fate instead? He imagined the drifter didn't keep the best company. Maybe he just lost track of what day it was? How that man dressed and took care of himself, he couldn't imagine he had a watch or calendar in an office to help him keep track of appointments. Besides, who writes on a calendar, *"Meet Kid at Train to Kill Someone"* anyway?

He pushed himself from the train, lifted his BMX from the dirt and began the long ride home. When he arrived, like always, he rode through the side yard towards the back fence. He reached, pulling the string to unlatch the metal lock on the opposite side of the wooden planks. Just beyond the fence was a small, metal shed that housed tools for yard work, house repairs and a small bike rack. He pushed his BMX into the shed, shutting the sliding, metal doors behind him. At the back of his house was a sliding glass door that led to a modest dining room. An old, clunky wooden dining table sat in the middle of the room, with an entertainment center to one side against the white wall, a small kitchen on the other side of the room. A golden, polished set of lights hung from the ceiling over the dining room table, the cheap bulbs illuminating everything in sight. A long hallway that led to each bedroom sat just to the right of the dining room. Mitch slid the glass door open, stepping into the home. The lights in the house were on, yet the home was eerily quiet.

"Hello?" He shouted, shutting the glass door behind him. "Anyone home? Where is everyone?"

From down the hall, he heard a noise. A sort of clunk, like a piece of wooden furniture being pushed against drywall. Stopping at the hallway entrance, he peered down towards the master bedroom. The master bedroom–his parent's room–sat at the end of the long, dark corridor. He could see inside the bedroom from where he stood, a soft light emanating from within. Mitch walked slowly towards the open doorway, his right fingertips barely tickling the hallway wall as he moved.

"Hello?" He asked under his breath. "Everything OK in there?"

The house remained quiet, silence piercing his young ears. As he reached the doorway, he pressed his right hand against the door frame, stopping himself from fully entering.

"Mom? Dad?" He asked, his voice trembling.

Silence remained, though only momentarily. Until he heard a ruffle sound, followed by something horrific. Something that, even after everything he'd witnessed in those train cars, still sent the worst shiver through his body he'd ever felt.

"Mitch!" His mother shrieked, followed by another loud clunk as furniture crashed into the drywall again. "Run! Get your sister and *run*!"

He shot into the bedroom, his young body freezing in time at what he saw.

Slunk over the bed, his head hanging downward towards the brown, shag carpet was his father. His lifeless eyes staring straight through Mitch, his mouth agape, drips of crimson streaming down his face and dripping to the floor below. His father's throat was cut wide open, allowing his head to fall back unnaturally, as though it was about to tear completely from his shoulders.

Across the room, his mother fought with an intruder, the attacker's arms reaching from behind her, trying to cover her mouth as she screamed for Mitch to escape while he still could.

"Mom!" Mitch shouted, his voice cracking as he took a step towards her.

"Not so fucking fast, kid," A voice grumbled from behind her.

From around his mother's left shoulder, the drifter appeared, a smile wrapping his dirty face ear to ear. His evil eyes shined through the greasy hair that hung from his head, covering his face. When his right hand came from behind her, the knife Mitch knew all too well was pressed against her throat. Mitch watched his mother gasp for air, her body trembling to the point she could no longer control it.

She whispered. "Please, get your sister and–"

"Shut the fuck up!" The man yelled, digging the blade into her flesh.

A thin line of blood trickled from under the blade, dripping freely towards the collar of her shirt.

"You weren't supposed to see any of this, kid," The man said, his eyes flickering around the room. "Why don't you do as your mother said and get the *fuck* out of here?"

"Let her go, you piece of shit," Mitch grumbled through gritted teeth.

"Oh, no can do, kid," He said, licking his lips. "This job is just too good to pass up. Too lucrative. I mean, come on, kid! You're the one who told me about your parents! How your dad owned his own pharmacy, remember? I knew your house *had* to be fucking loaded."

"What is he saying?" His mother whimpered.

"Shut *up!*" He screamed again. "Kid, turn around, and get the fuck outta here."

"Not a fucking chance," Mitch barked back.

"Fine," The drifter said. "You want to see all of this happen? We can do it your way."

He slid the blade across Mitch's mother's throat, cutting deep as he went. Her eyes shot wide open as she began gasping for air to stay alive. When he let her go, her body dropped to the carpet. She wrapped her hands around her throat, those gasps turning to low gurgles as the crimson liquid filled her mouth, her body giving out as she choked on her own warm blood.

"No! Mom!" Mitch screamed, his voice cracking.

"Now it's your turn," The drifter said, licking his lips. "Let's fucking do this."

Mitch seethed with rage as his little feet took off towards him. His body crashed into the man's, as he reached with both arms to get the knife from his thin, demonic looking hands. He held on to the man's wrist when he attempted to swing the blade down into his young body.

"You little shit," He grunted. "I'm going to fucking *end you!*"

Mitch pushed the drifter's right arm into the air, trying to kick at him, but it was no use. The man grabbed Mitch by the back of his hair, tossing him across the room, forcing Mitch to crash land on his back. When Mitch attempted to jump to his feet, the man was there, ready for his feeble attempt at fighting back. He drove the knife into Mitch's ribcage faster than a snakebite, tearing it from his flesh. Mitch shrieked as blood spurted from the wound. He pressed his hands over the gash, taking a couple steps back in agonizing pain. The drifter grabbed him by the sides of his head, forcing him to look into his eyes.

"I told you, I don't enjoy killing kids. But if I have to, so be it."

He pulled the kid's head towards his chest, then shoved it away, forcing it to crash hard onto the sharp end of his parent's dresser. Mitch was immediately knocked out cold, his body falling to the ground like a sack of yard waste. Blood continued to pour from the stab in his side and now pooled underneath his head.

The man wiped the sweat and spittle from his lips as he exited the room. From behind a closed door down the hall, a baby was crying. He pushed the door open so hard, the handle stuck in the drywall behind it. Sitting in a crib was Mitch's baby sister, Myrna. She wailed and wailed, terrified and unaware of the horror that had occurred just a few feet away. He stepped to the crib, brushing his hand over the top of her head.

"Good luck, little girl," He whispered. "Your life is going to be fucked up beyond words."

He left the room, returning to the scene where three bodies laid, bleeding out, dead or dying in their own respective ways. It was then that he ransacked the house, taking anything and everything of value—jewelry, wads of cash from Mr. Graves' safe and two sets of keys that hung in the kitchen. When he was satisfied, he left out the back, sliding glass door. He ran across the backyard, hopped over the back fence and disappeared into the night.

Mitch remained on the carpet, bleeding from his head and ribs. As though the stars above had aligned just right, or maybe he wasn't completely out of luck as he'd imagined, his eyes popped open, his lungs expanding, hoping to fill with oxygen. When he pressed his hands into the carpet, his arms quivered as he pushed himself to all fours. He briefly glanced back at his mother, lying on the floor, lifeless. She looked just like the rag doll bodies he'd seen at the train tracks. The lifeless lumps he'd himself helped create. He looked away, covering his eyes as he tried to lift his body, shielding himself from the horror he himself invited into their home. When he finally got to his feet, he sauntered down the hall to Myrna. Her crying pierced the silence in the home, letting him know she was alive. He lifted her from the crib, her body becoming covered in the blood that now poured from his own. Holding his baby sister in his trembling arms, he walked her to the front door. Once outside, he took Myrna to the street, and slowly lowered his body to sit on the curb in front of their family home. He held her in his trembling arms, as his fluids flooded from his body, gathering on the sidewalk underneath him. She cried and cried in absolute fear as he held her against his chest, shushing and promising that somehow, someday, he would make everything OK.

CHAPTER 14

16 Years Later...

The sun burned in the hot and clear summer sky, drenching the city of Thousand Oaks, California in gorgeous oranges and golds. The only reprieve from its harsh rays, a sweet, cool breeze that blew throughout the valley. A welcomed yet subtle reminder of spring as it transformed into the unrelenting summer. Nestled on the outskirts of town was Tarantula Hill High, an old-fashioned style high school building which sat within the shadows underneath Tarantula Hill on old Gainsborough Road. Tarantula Hill High, with its pale concrete walls, loomed high, casting shadows over the main courtyard out front. The two story building housed every classroom indoors, each class window glistening in the summer sun. A staircase led the way from the courtyard to the main entrance, the word *ADMINISTRATION* in light blue metal sitting just above the front doors. On either side of the stairs was a wide ledge, each adorned with a light blue, retro style lamp post. A concrete pathway led through the courtyard towards a circular driveway made of asphalt, serving its purpose perfectly for drop off and pick up each day. Fresh, green grass rested on either side of the walkway with a bike rack set to the right. A rusting relic from long ago rarely used these days.

The last day of school was finally upon the students of Tarantula Hill High. That afternoon, students poured through the double doorway just as the bell chimed, ringing and echoing off the hills in the distance. From a few random windows on the second floor, papers had been thrown, the pages fluttering through the air towards the concrete and grass below. Scattered all around, feet stomped over them as students ran about the courtyard, high-fiving one another and saying their goodbyes until fall, when they'd all return to the halls of Tarantula Hill High. It was almost as though, if you listened carefully enough, you might think that *School's Out* from Alice Cooper was playing somewhere off in the distance, the hard rock tune floating through the air like rock n roll butterflies fluttering along with the breeze.

Bursting through the doorways was 16-year-old Myrna Graves. She cut through the crowded entrance as though she was parting the sea with her mere presence. Her dyed, black hair tied back into a flowing ponytail, two thick strands hanging downward and hiding her face from her classmates. She wore a faded and torn Motorhead tee, with a black-and-white striped long sleeve underneath. A pair of fishnets appeared from underneath a pair of black, cutoff denim shorts, stretching her legs and disappearing into a pair of worn out Doc Martens. Her thick, black eyeliner was applied in a rush, and it was clear she didn't give a shit.

"Have a great summer, Myrna," A blonde girl shouted, stopping her just as she hit the top step. A sarcastic smile wrapped her face as she looked towards a friend sitting next to her.

"Yeah," Her friend said with a laugh. "Enjoy returning to your *bat* cave for the summer. Weirdo."

Both blonde girls were cookie-cutter versions of one another. Golden hair resting on their shoulders, their thin bodies wrapped in school spirit gear. They sat together on one ledge that overlooked the courtyard. Myrna swung around, shooting both a glare that would've paired perfectly with homicide.

"Awww, thanks, Amanda!" Myrna said, matching the blonde's sarcasm. "That's so kind of you. Enjoy being out on your rich, asshole daddy's boat. I hope you don't get thrown overboard and sucked into the propeller."

"Geez, Myrna," Amanda said, a look of disgust on her young face. "Take a pill, would ya?"

"Take a joke," Sherri chimed in, equally grossed out.

"Sorry, did I offend you both?" She asked, her hand up to her chest in pretend sorrow. She quickly shifted back to her teenage angst. "Too bad. I hope you both *rot* this summer. You fucking pair of clown shoes."

She turned away, bouncing down the stairs as a chorus of *how dare you* from both girls tried to catch up to her from behind. She moved with a confident swagger towards the parking lot, a middle finger held high into the air for both of them.

"Myrna!" An adult voice cut through the noise of the students. "That's inappropriate, get back here!"

Standing at the top of the steps was one of the many teachers, her hands on her hips in disapproval.

"Sorry, Mrs. McKean," She shouted without turning around, not breaking stride. "Schools out, can't bust me."

Stomping across the courtyard, her eyes scanned through the crowd towards the pickup area in front of the school. When it was clear she'd found what–or who–she was looking for, she stopped. A sly smile appeared on her face as she shook her head before continuing the short walk towards the mass of cars that awaited the students. Standing on the curb, leaned way back against a car stood her older brother, Mitch, now 30-years-old. Mitch, dressed in a pair of tight fitting black jeans, a black t-shirt covered by a dark blue jacket with a pair of aviator glasses hiding his eyes, stood clapping and shaking his head in Myrna's direction. A look upon his face as though he was beaming with pride at the display he'd just seen.

"Well done, Sis," He said as she reached him. "Well done. I can see you haven't lost any of your patented charm."

"What the hell is this?" She asked, ignoring the comment. She nodded her head at his car.

"Oh, you like it?" He asked, removing his aviators, standing up straight. "I just bought it. Pretty sick, huh?"

"*Sick?* What year is it? 1997? Did you buy a new 311 CD the same day?"

"Hilarious. This car doesn't have a CD player though."

"It's good to know your sense of humor hasn't dried up, brother," She said.

Mitch showed off his new car as though he was a presenter at a vehicle trade show. A brand new Zeus-X1. The latest and greatest in electric vehicle technology. And anyone who desired to drive one would have to pay a pretty penny to do so. Zeus-X1's looked like spaceships on wheels. Slick, stylized bodies that sat low to the street, equipped with state-of-the-art technology under the hood and touch screens everywhere inside which controlled everything for the car. Mitch's Zeus was the same, dark blue color as the jacket he currently wore.

"Look, do you like it or not?" He finally asked, getting more serious this time.

"Yeah, it's cool."

"*Cool?* That's all you have to say? That it's *cool?*"

"What do you want me to say, Mitch? It's a car."

"It's *so not* just a car, Myrna. This is *the* car. Top of the line. All electric, which I figured you'd enjoy. And it's fast as shit."

"Be honest. Did you buy that jacket to match the car?" She asked, ignoring his comment yet again. Something Mitch had grown used to over the last 16 years. "Or do you only own dark blue tops so you can always match?"

"Very funny," He said, opening the passenger door. "Just get in, would ya? And happy birthday, by the way."

"Why thank you, Brother," She smiled. "Wait, where's my present?"

"You get to ride in the new car. Isn't that enough?"

"Come on, give me a break. Really. What did you get me?"

"Get in the car and I'll tell you all about it."

"Wait, you're going to *tell me* about my present? Can't I just open it like, oh, I don't know, every other present ever given in history?"

"This is a different type of present, Myrna," He said, a sly, yet confusing look washing over his face. "Just get in. I'm taking you to lunch and I'll explain everything."

"Alright," She said with a deep sigh and a shrug. "But this *better* be good."

She took her seat as he slammed the door. Walking around the back of the car, he made his way back to the driver's side.

"Oh, it's good," He whispered to himself, replacing his aviator glasses. He opened the door and said to himself before jumping in. "It's something you've wished for all your life."

CHAPTER 15

Mitch and Myrna sat across from one another at a plastic picnic table on the patio of Electric Burger and Cone, a tiny food stand just outside of downtown Thousand Oaks. The picnic table's steel legs remained caked with shrapnel thanks to years upon years of torment from families grabbing a quick bite to eat and teenager's spending countless hours after school wolfing down double burgers and vanilla milkshakes. Electric Burger and Cone didn't take up much space on the corner of Westlake Boulevard, the same spot where it stood serving greasy flat top burgers, french fries and assorted ice cream treats for close to 40 years. Even as the rest of the neighborhood continued to grow and modernize, Electric Burger and Cone remained true to its original roots. A small shack like building with no indoor seating, a walkup window serving as the only way to order. Its wooden roof had seen better days, and the tall sign that shot high into the sky had stopped spinning years ago. Though its longtime mascot Sparky–a lightning bolt with human-like features–still illuminated on top when the sun went down. Sparky held his trademark double cheeseburger and a waffle cone, the soft serve in a perfect spiral. The windows were plastered with sun bleached posters that offered different daily specials, though, from their appearance, it would appear that the specials hadn't changed in quite some time.

Myrna sat sideways on the bench, both feet up with her legs tucked into her body as she savored a chocolate dipped vanilla cone. Across from her, Mitch chewed away unabashedly at a double cheeseburger with bacon, french fries dumped onto the burger's yellow wrapper with a paper cup of soft drink weeping condensation from the ice cold beverage inside. He took a bite, dropping the burger before tearing away at a packet of ketchup, promptly emptying it onto the wax wrapper for dipping.

"So, you enjoying your birthday lunch?" He asked, chewing rudely as he spoke.

"Lunch?" She asked, glaring at him out of the tops of her eyes. "You call this lunch? An ice cream cone?"

"Hey, I said you could order *anything* you wanted. *You* chose an ice cream cone. What do you want me to do, beg you to eat?" He dipped three fries at a time in the ketchup, devouring them like they were his prey.

"A Sparky Burger with fries? That's what you call lunch? No thanks. You know I don't eat this kind of stuff."

"You could do much worse than a Sparky Burger with fries, you know?"

"And yet, we could still do so much better," She said, snark in her voice.

"Look," Mitch said, wiping his face and dropping a napkin with purpose, like he could slam it onto the table for effect. "You know this place. It's important to me. Shit, I thought it was important to the both of us, but I guess I was wrong."

Myrna rolled her eyes as she shook her head. She took another lick of her frozen treat, the soft serve dripping down the cone towards her black painted fingernails. She looked around the eating area, customers as scarce as ever. The air filled with the sound of cars as they shot by at ridiculous speeds, the sun's rays beating down upon them.

"I mean," Mitch said, slurping at his soft drink. "When we first moved here to live with Grandma after our parents died, this is where she took us to eat. Like, all the time, Myrna."

"I was a baby then, dude," She barked. "I don't have the fond memories of this place like you do. Besides, our parents didn't just *die*, Mitch. They were brutally murdered. You were almost murdered along with them, or do you only remember things that are covered in American cheese and secret sauce?"

"Hey, *great things* come covered in American cheese and secret sauce. I'll be damned if I'm going to sit here and let you talk badly about American cheese and secret sauce."

"Yeah, yeah." She said, waving him off.

"And of course I remember our parents. *I was there.* I lived it," He shouted. He lowered his voice, composing his emotions. "Anyway, I'm sorry if I was wrong about lunch. OK? I thought this place was, like, *our* place? You know?"

Myrna remained silent, just staring at her boots. She felt bad that she had minimized his memories of greasy fast food. If it meant that much to him, maybe she needed to embrace it a bit more. If for nothing else, his sake. And if she were being honest, aside from their grandmother who had taken them in, she had little else in terms of family. Mitch was her brother. He might be a bit much, what, with his matching jacket and car, but he was hers and hers alone.

"How dare you question my memory of that day. Of course I remember. I remember it like it happened yesterday. There isn't a day that goes by that I don't think about what happened. How I could've helped or, I don't know, stopped him."

"Stopped him?" She laughed. A hard, belly laugh at this suggestion. "How could you have stopped him? You were 14 years old. I've seen pictures of you. You were a scrawny little punk. Hell, I could've probably kicked your ass if we were both 14."

"Yeah, well," Mitch said, clicking his tongue as though he was trying to remove a rogue piece of beef from his teeth. "I don't know about all that. If we're going to spend the summer together, do you think we could stop arguing already?"

"Whatever," She said, adjusting her sitting position slightly. "Man, I wish I would've been there that day. You know, the age I am now? I would've fought that piece of shit off. I would've killed him myself."

"Funny you should say that," Mitch said with a smirk, wiping his lips with a napkin, crumbling it into a ball and tossing it into a trash can a few feet away. "That brings me to your *real* birthday present."

"My *real* birthday present? What does that mean? I get more than a cone from a crappy burger stand?"

"Again, careful about the burger stand. I love this place. And yes, I have an actual birthday present for you, believe it or not."

They remained silent for a moment, a real shit-eating grin covering Mitch's face.

"Well, out with it already," She shouted, shoving her legs under the picnic table to face her brother. "Don't keep me waiting!"

"My present to you, my sweet Myrna, *is*," He tapped his index fingers on the table in a faux drumroll. "Is *him*." He held his hands out, palms up, showcasing not a thing.

Myrna's eyes jumped back and forth from palm to palm, as confusion in her mind grew at a feverish pace. She felt lost in that moment by what he had said, and the lack of what he had actually presented to her. No tangible object, no explanation even. Just that word. *Him.*

"What does that mean, exactly? Him?" She asked, her eyebrows reaching towards the sky.

"Haven't you been saying your whole life how you want to do that? How you want to kill him? That is what I am giving to you. I am giving you *him*."

"I think Sparky needs to change the oil on that fryer, you've been poisoned," She said, shaking her head.

"No Myrna, listen–"

"I am listening, and it doesn't make any sense dude!"

"Just listen!" He shouted. "We're spending the summer together, right? It was my suggestion, remember?"

"That's only because I got into a little bit of trouble and Grandma called you. She just pawned me off onto you."

A few months back, Myrna and her best–and only–friend, Deirdre, had found themselves in some hot water. A party was being thrown at one of the popular kids homes one weekend, and Myrna and Deirdre played the role of party crashers. The girl's name was Jasmine and her parents were out of town on business, or something like that. Myrna didn't care the reason. When they arrived at the massive home way out on Falling Star Lane, they couldn't believe what they saw. The house was littered with expensive items–luxurious furniture, trinkets of gold, *real* gold. Even a crystal chandelier hung above the entryway. It didn't take a detective to realize her parents were loaded. Not long after their arrival, the popular kids had Myrna and her friend ejected from the party. They weren't part of the inclusive, hip crowd, and their attendance wasn't welcome. Though, a few days later, Jasmine's parents found out about the unauthorized soiree. Not because of any leftover booze bottles floating in the pool or half smoked joints in the gardenias. A priceless necklace had gone missing. The necklace boasted a thick band made of pure gold, and emblazoned in some of the biggest diamonds you'd ever seen. Not to be outmatched, a gigantic blue diamond would have rested perfectly on the chest of anyone lucky enough to wear it. Needless to say, Jasmine's parents were furious beyond words. A priceless artifact missing amongst the teenage chaos. It wasn't long before the police were involved, and they set their sights directly onto Myrna and Deirdre. Unfortunately for the parents, the necklace never surfaced, and any accusations couldn't be proven. Though, her parents, as well as the rest of the town, always held their suspicions against the two unwelcomed girls. While they got off without punishment from the law, the jury of public scrutiny had their way with them. And Jasmine's parents still to this day believed that Myrna had stolen the priceless jewelry. An accusation which they refused to let go.

"That's besides the point," Mitch said, shutting her down. "It was still my suggestion. And why do you think I suggested it?"

"I haven't the slightest idea, dude."

"Look, I may have gotten a little ahead of myself. There's something that I need to tell you. Something I need to come clean about that I've been hiding from you and everyone else in my life for a really long time."

"Can you just spill it already?"

"Now, this could be a lot to take. And it might be hard to hear, but once I explain everything, it will all make sense."

"Just fucking *tell me!*" She shouted in a pretend, crying tone. Her patience wearing paper thin.

He removed his aviator sunglasses then let out a deep, trembling sigh before he spoke. "I'm a killer, Myrna."

CHAPTER 16

Myrna remained speechless, staring deep into the eyes of her older brother. His admission shocked her. She didn't know what to even make of those words. *I'm a killer, Myrna.* Together, they sat emotionless, still and silent. Mitch sat with bated breath, hoping for any response from his younger sister. As time continued to tick away, he became more and more nervous of what her response might be. And when it came, it wasn't even in the same universe as what he'd expected of her.

Myrna burst into laughter. Her body fell back, her face tilted towards the sky. Deep, throaty *HAs* erupted from her wide open mouth, her eyes welling with tears as though this was easily the funniest joke she'd ever heard. When her body lurched forward, she pounded her open palm onto the plastic tabletop, rattling the leftover food and wrappers like an earthquake was shaking beneath their feet.

"I'm serious, Myrna," He said in almost a whisper. "I'm not kidding around."

"Right," She said through her boisterous laughter. "A killer? *You're* a killer? You couldn't kill a moth. I mean, look at you. Your hands are smoother than mine."

"OK," He said, replacing his sunglasses. "You get it out of your system yet? This is serious."

"Right, right," She said, wiping the tears from her eyes. "Go ahead. *Go on*, tell me about all the people you've killed, brother. Please. I can't wait to hear about it."

"First of all, keep your voice down. I don't want anyone to hear us talking about this. It's a sensitive subject."

"Sure, Brother," She whispered, her laughter continuing. "I'll keep my voice down."

"I've been killing since I was, let's just say, a teenager. I don't know why I have that urge, but I do. It's something I need to do. Something I'm good at. And I enjoy doing it."

"Mitch, come on."

"It's true, Myrna."

He stopped himself momentarily, tapping his fingers on the table as his brain ran circles in his skull. Mitch knew he couldn't—and shouldn't—expose too much about how he'd learned to kill, or who taught him the tricks of the trade. Myrna may never forgive him if she knew the man who showed him the ropes killed their parents. That conversation would have to wait for another day.

"I met a man. A drifter. He was a killer, and he took me under his wing. Taught me how to kill and how to get away with it. He opened something within my brain that I didn't even know existed until that point."

"Yeah, OK," She said, wiping her hands on her denim shorts, looking over her shoulder, uninterested.

"Alright, wise ass. Let me ask you this. If I'm lying right now, how do you think I live the way I do? Drive the cars I drive? Wear nice clothes and have a great apartment?"

"Dude, I don't know. Look, can we stop this already? It's really too much. Let's get outta here. This bench is hurting my ass."

"It's because I kill for money, Myrna," He whispered, leaning his body over the table towards her. As he did, he tore the sunglasses from his face so she could see his eyes. The seriousness that burned within them.

Myrna's expression changed. In an instant, she went from finding this entire exchange slightly comical, to understanding the severity of what

Mitch was saying. Slowly, she turned her head back to her brother, staring deep into his eyes.

"You're not kidding, are you?"

"No, Myrna," He said, sitting back. "That's what I've been trying to tell you. I've always been a killer. It's in me, somehow. But, unlike most drifters and shitheels that kill for fun, I found a way to profit from it. I turned my passion into a career, Myrna. I work for a family with mafia ties. They pay me to clean up their unwanted shit. And they pay me *a lot*."

"So, why are you telling me all of this? *Now*, of all times? On my *birthday*, you decide to share this *insane* news with me?"

"That's what I've been trying to get at," He said, a smile washing over his face. "I recently met another hired gun that works for this family. Just take *one* guess who that man was."

"I don't know," She said with a shrug. "Seymour Butts?"

"You're hysterical," He said, shaking his head. "I met the man that killed our parents."

Myrna's felt as though her world came to a screeching halt. Like everything around her fell into slow motion. She felt sick to her stomach, dizzy from this admission. It was all too much to handle. Luckily, she hadn't scarfed down a double burger and fries like her brother had. If so, all of that lunch might be deposited right back onto that table top.

"Wait, hold the fucking phone," She said, attempting to right the ship in her mind. "You're telling me you met the piece of shit who killed our mom and dad?"

"That's exactly what I'm telling you."

"How did you know it was him? How could you be so certain?"

"Trust me," He said, his voice somber and low. "I know it was him."

"*Trust* you? Trust someone who's telling me he's a trained, hired hitman for a mafia family? Are you *serious*, Mitch? How can you seriously believe I would trust you right now?"

"Hey, watch it. I may be a killer, but I'm still your big brother. Have I ever steered you wrong? Have I ever done wrong by you?"

He was right. Mitch might in fact be a murderer. The jury within Myrna's mind was still out on this one. But, he was her big brother. And in her entire life as far back as she could remember, all he'd ever done was his best to take care of her. To be there for her. Even when he'd moved out of their grandma's place, he always showed up on birthdays, to recitals, to be a shoulder for her to cry on when whomever she was dating was mean to her, and always at the ready to bail her out of trouble. He'd always done the right thing for Myrna. It was as though he lived to be there for her, no matter what. This didn't ease her stomach at all. He was still a killer. And as much as she loved him, at that moment, she was terrified of him all the same.

"So, what then?"

"For your birthday present, my gift to you is that we, you and I, *together*, will find him and kill him."

"Find him and kill him? *That's* your gift to me? To commit murder with you?"

"It's what you've always wanted. To get back at this motherfucker. To end his life. Believe me, it's all I've ever wanted, too."

"You know, My Chemical Romance reunited and are touring again. Couldn't you just get us tickets to go see them? That would be a *much* better gift if you ask me."

"No. Forget the tickets," He said, shuffling in his seat. "Come on, it'll be perfect. You and I, *together*, getting revenge on this scumbag?"

"Three cheers for sweet revenge, huh?"

"What the fuck does that mean?" He asked. "Come on, be serious. What do you say?"

"I say," She sat quietly for a moment. Not as though she was actually thinking this proposition over. Was she? She couldn't believe it. "No. *No*, Mitch. I don't think so. I'm not a *killer*. Come on, dude."

"What?" He was stunned. "I thought you'd love this idea."

"You thought I'd love *murder*? Do you know me at *all*?"

"Well, I mean, look at you," He said, scanning her up and down. "You're into all that dark, horror shit."

"That's fucking fiction," She shouted. She threw her hands throughout the air in front of his face as though she was having a seizure and spoke in a mocking tone. "*Fiction*, you twit."

"Well, one way or another, that piece of shit dies this summer," He said, collecting any trash from the table. "I'm going to find him and kill him. And either you're in it with me, or you're not."

"OK, the answer is simple," She said, standing from the table. "I'm *not*."

"Myrna, we have to do this together. It's just the way it has to be."

"Whatever, Mitch."

"Besides, we've got a good amount of drive time to discuss this. Just trust me, alright? It's something that we need to do."

"You sure we can't just go see My Chemical Romance instead? It would be a lot more fun than murder."

"Spoken like someone who's never watched life fade from someone's eyes," He said, patting her on the back. "No, forget My Chemical Romance. I promise, you'll enjoy this so much more."

Myrna hung her head as they marched together towards the car. Mitch kept his hand secured upon the top of her back as they walked, opening the car door for her to enter. A proud smile remained on his face as he looked around the street, taking in a deep breath of fresh, summer air. He opened his own door, jumped into the car, and in no time, they were off. They hit the 23 Freeway driving north. Headed to a destiny that made Myrna's stomach turn. An unknown place that she now dreaded. But deep in her gut, it was Mitch, and she knew she trusted him. She had to trust him. And, what shocked her more, was that in that deep down place where trust resided, she felt a small tingling of excitement. It was as though Mitch had lit a fire inside her soul she didn't know even existed. A pilot light of hate, fury and revenge, and a desire burned within her body in a way she'd never experienced before.

CHAPTER 17

Myrna remained deathly quiet as they blazed the 5 Freeway heading North. The initial plan was to drive from Thousand Oaks to Sacramento, stay a night to charge their batteries–their own as well as the car's–before continuing their path towards its bloody ending. She was still anything but sure of what her brother had shared with her. Her brother? A killer? Of course she found it hard to believe. In a circumstance such as this, it's easy to be skeptical. Especially when you know someone as well as she knew Mitch. Or, as well as she imagined she did. Keeping her eyes locked out the passenger window, she watched as they passed through absolute nothingness through Central California. Different cities with unknown names blurred by as they sped past. To cut the boredom of the drive, Myrna took it upon herself to count just how many Chili's restaurants sat between Thousand Oaks and Sacramento. Once she hit double digits, she lost count, as keeping track made the boredom so much worse. Just as she began considering opening the door, allowing her body to roll out along the speeding asphalt below to escape, Mitch cut the silence.

"Do you want to talk about the incident?" He asked, glancing in her direction, then back to the road ahead.

"What incident?" She asked, lifting her tired head. She rested her elbow against the door, her balled fist pressed hard into her cheek.

"You know what I mean," He said, expecting her to read his mind. "The incident. Where you and your friend robbed that house. What was that all about?"

"We didn't rob any house, Mitch," She snapped. "I told you already. Shit, I've told everybody *so many times*. We didn't steal that necklace or those diamonds. It's just a huge misunderstanding."

"I don't know, Myrna. It just seems weird that you two were even there."

"Where? At a *party*? Geez, dude. You're not *that* old, are you? That's what kids my age do. They go to parties. They crash parties. Kids drink, have fun. Maybe you should try it sometime."

"I, I have fun," He stuttered, as though he was trying to convince Myrna and himself at the same time. "What you don't seem to remember is that when I was your age, I was home all the time. I was there with you. To take care of you and help Grandma around the house. I didn't have time for parties."

"Just because you didn't have time, does that mean I shouldn't have fun, either? Come on. I didn't do anything wrong, seriously. Can we please just drop this?"

"Alright, alright," He finally conceded.

"Let's put some music on, what do you say?"

"Uh," He muttered, scanning the rear-view mirror, changing lanes. "Sure. What do you want to hear? I've got satellite radio in here. If you flick through the screen, you can check my presets."

"Presets?" She laughed. "No, no presets. And no satellite radio. Here, I'll choose something."

Myrna fished her phone from the back pocket of her cut-off jeans, flicking through the screen a moment. She reached towards the console, plugging the white cord that hung from the robotic looking screen into the bottom of her smartphone. Soon, the sludgy, chugging cords of *Static Age* from the Misfits began pounding through the car's speakers, followed by that iconic shouting and screaming. *STATIC! STATIC! STATIC!*

Myrna rested in her chair, a smile washed across her happy, goth face.

"Oh, god," Mitch muttered, turning the volume down considerably. "Do we have to listen to this shit? It's so hectic. I can barely concentrate."

"Are you kidding? This is classic!"

"As classic as it may be, it's hard to focus with that screaming. And the sound is so damn poor. It's not 1987, Myrna."

"It's punk rock, dude. It's not supposed to be polished and pretty. God, didn't you learn anything as a kid?"

"While you're wasting time on punk records and horror movies, I was being taught a very different education, Myrna."

"Oh, right. I forgot. *Homicide.*"

"Don't make fun of me. I was being serious. It took a lot to tell you that."

"Right."

Mitch adjusted himself in his seat, his eyes rolling like they were caught in a cement mixer. He scanned the road, checked his mirrors.

"I don't listen to this kind of stuff, that's all. I get my–," He raised his balled fist into the air, letting out a deep, guttural grunt. "My aggressions out in different ways. So when I listen to music, I want it to be relaxing."

"OK, fine," Myrna said, turning off the searing sound of the Misfits. "What do you want to hear, Brother?"

"Do you like Hall and Oates? *I* like Hall and Oates."

"Hall and Oates?" She let out another deep laugh. "You are such a *dad.* It's so gross!"

"OK," He said, nodding his head. "Fine, play whatever you want. You know what? I don't even care."

"No, stop it," She said through giggles, flicking through her phone. "We can listen to Hall and Oates. It's fine. This trip is about you teaching me, remember? Let's add music to the list. Besides, what's the travel plan exactly? Where is this son of a bitch hiding anyway?"

"That son of a bitch is currently hiding in a place called Eureka, California," He replied, clicking on his turn signal, switching lanes again to pass a truck.

"Alright then, Eureka, here we come!"

"Ah, not quite. We need to make a stop or two before that. Sorry, I've got some obligations to fulfill on this trip."

"What the fuck, Mitch? I thought this entire thing was about you and me? Getting revenge or whatever you want to call it."

"Don't worry, it is," He said, patting her on the thigh a couple times. A little too hard for her comfort. "First, I need to take care of a job in Reno. It should net me a cool 40 thousand, though."

"40 thousand *dollars*? Are you fucking serious?"

"I told you, I handle serious business for very important people," He looked over his right shoulder, checking clearance to switch lanes yet again.

Myrna's face transformed, showcasing a look like her brother's business impressed her. 40 thousand dollars? That seemed like an entirely different galaxy to Myrna. Even saying the words 40 thousand dollars was foreign. To her, when he mentioned that kind of money, he may as well be speaking another language.

"So, tonight we'll stop in Sacramento to sleep and get some rest. Then tomorrow, I'll get us checked into a small motel in Reno. I'll handle my business while you're asleep, and when you wake up all bright eyed and bushy tailed, we'll be ready to hit the road towards Eureka."

"What is this," She swallowed hard. Unsure if she wanted to know at all. "This job of yours? You know, in Reno?"

"The less you know about that, probably the better," He said with a sly grin and a wink.

"OK," She nodded. "And the less you wink at me is probably for the better, too. You fucking weirdo."

She thumbed through her phone some more, finally pressing play on some Hall and Oates. Mitch forced the gas pedal down, gaining immense speed as the opening to *Rich Girl* poured from the speakers.

CHAPTER 18

The warm sun of the day had turned in for the night, allowing the moon to come out to play as Mitch turned into the parking lot of the Sac-Time Motel. A two-story motor inn close to the Sacramento Airport nestled on the corner of Watt Avenue and Longview Drive. The blue pole adorned with chipping paint shot high into the sky, topped with a square light box flickering fluorescent behind a logo of a cartoon piece of luggage asleep with a comforter pulled to its face. The marquee just underneath the flickering sign boasted of Free HBO, Wi-Fi and weekly rates. Myrna squinched her face as they pulled in, parking directly in front of one of the blue painted doorways.

"Alright, home sweet home," Mitch said, opening the door and exiting the vehicle.

Myrna remained in the car for a moment, thinking that he must be joking. When the driver door slammed shut, she realized her fears were way too real. This must be where they'd be staying for the evening. Slowly she opened the door, stepping onto the cracking asphalt parking lot. At the far end of the lot, Myrna saw an older man with an equally old woman standing together. He wore a white tank top and swim trunks. Her, in an oversized tee and shorts. They both chugged away at their own bottles of wine, sucking down cigarettes.

"We're seriously staying here tonight?" She asked, the tone in her voice unmistakable.

"Yeah, what's the big deal?" Mitch asked, lifting a duffle bag from the trunk.

"Didn't you say you had 40 thousand? Why are we staying at this roach motel?"

"Hey, first, keep your voice down. Don't throw that kind of number into the air. The people that hang in hotels like this can sniff that kind of information from miles away. They're like sharks. And dollar bills are chum in the water."

"Shouldn't that be enough to sway you from staying here?"

"No, not at all. This place is inconspicuous. Cops don't come to motels like this looking for people like you and me. And second, before I was *rudely* interrupted," He said, motioning to her backpack in the trunk.

Myrna reached in, throwing her bag over her right shoulder.

"It's only for one night. It's just a place to crash and catch some rest. We're not here to sightsee. We have a job to do. *I* have multiple jobs to do. Tonight we can get some dinner and get a good night's sleep and we'll be out of here at sunrise."

"Damn. I had no idea this trip would be *so much fun*. Thanks for the birthday trip, Brother. Why wasn't I *more* excited to come with you?"

"You may enjoy throwing around the angst filled attitude now," He said, slamming the trunk hatch. "But trust me, in a few days, you'll *actually* be thanking me. When I make your biggest dream come true. When you get *him*."

"Right. When I get *him*."

Together, they entered the main office of the motel and were immediately hit in the nose by the lingering stench of moldy carpet, stale coffee and ages old dust that swirled throughout the air. A chubby man sat behind the counter flicking away at a smartphone, playing a game with the volume at full blast. At first, he paid them no attention, choosing to finish the round of whatever game he focused on over delivering quality service to his new customers.

"Excuse me," Mitch finally said, leaning onto the counter.

The man held up a finger, his mouth agape as though that game was the most important thing in his life. A noise chimed through the air that sounded to Mitch and Myrna as though his turn had just come to an abrupt halt. He pounded his fist onto the counter, rubbed it across his sweaty head, and finally shot them a smile.

"Sorry about that. How can I help the two of you?"

"Need a room for the night. A double queen, if available," Mitch said.

"But Hun," Myrna chimed in. "Do we *really* need two beds?"

"What?" Mitch asked, his face, disapproving. "Shut up, Myrna. Two beds, please."

"Fine, two beds it is," She said. "We can switch between the two of them."

"Myrna," He whispered under his breath.

The man stared at the two of them, and, if his expression said anything, he didn't have a clue what was unfolding before him.

"Like he said, two beds, *please* sir," Myrna looked towards her brother with bright, wide-open eyes. She returned her stare to the man behind the counter. "You see, we're lovers." She wrapped her arms around Mitch's right arm.

"Get off of me," Mitch shot back, tearing his arm from her. "Ignore her, please."

"It's our honeymoon. Tomorrow we fly out to Cabo," She said, clicking her tongue and batting her eyes.

"Shut up, Myrna," He whispered, shaking his head.

"Uh, yeah, OK," The man said. "You're in room 109. Two queen beds. Please, uh, sign here, sir."

Mitch signed the paperwork, pushing it back towards the man.

"The pool closes at 10PM, and we serve breakfast until 9am each morning," The man said, stuffing the cash Mitch handed over into a drawer. "Two keys or one?"

"Oh, just one," Myrna said with a coy smile. "We won't be leaving the room much, if you get my drift."

"One is fine," Mitch replied, tucking the key into his back pocket.

Mitch remained a step or two ahead of Myrna as they walked the path towards their room on the first floor. Behind him, she snickered to herself at his discomfort.

"You found that funny, huh?" He asked, not turning around.

"Oh, come on, you wet blanket. I'm just playing around."

"Well," He tucked the keycard into the door lock, removing it quickly. The green light lit, allowing them to enter. "I didn't find it funny. Not at all."

"Get a sense of humor, dumbbell," She said, following him inside. "You have to let me have *some* fun on this trip."

"Well, I hope it's out of your system. We have a lot of business to attend to in the next few days."

He flicked the light and Myrna was almost certain she saw something scurry from the shadows across the floor. Two beds sat, a nightstand between them with a gold plated lamp on top next to an old, rotary telephone. Its plastic stained from years of use, abuse, and from the smell of the place, mass amounts of cigarette smoke that had come and gone. The blankets on each bed were a horrible maroon, with a terrible floral pattern Myrna assumed must have matched the carpet at some point in time. On the opposite side of the room sat a large wooden dresser covered in stains. The newest item in the room, a flat panel television on top of the dresser. At the far end of the room, a white countertop with a sink, and a doorway that led to the bathroom.

"See? Not so bad now, is it?" Mitch asked.

He tossed his duffel bag onto the bed closest to the door, taking a seat at the end. Myrna walked past without saying a word, dropping her backpack on the next bed. Taking a seat on the edge, with her index finger she pushed the phone with her eyebrows raised.

"Geez. I don't know if I've ever seen one of these before."

"Oh, yeah. Hotels still think it's important to have those things. Don't think I've ever found the need to use one."

Myrna pushed herself back, landing on the bed. She pushed her body upwards so her head landed on one pillow, stretching her hands underneath her neck to prop her head. Mitch shuffled through his duffel bag, removing a few items of clothing–fresh socks, a different jacket, a pair of jeans. Myrna shot up, returning to the edge of the bed as Mitch pulled a revolver and a box of bullets from the bag, setting them on the bed next to him. The pistol appeared spotless, sending rays of light over the walls from its steel casing as the street light cut through the stained blinds over the window. With a handle made of old, polished wood, the pistol was silver with gold letters stamped into the barrel. Myrna could see the letters A and L pressed in shining gold.

"Mitch, what the fuck!?" She shouted.

"What?" He asked, a stupefied look on his face.

"Why do you have that? A fucking *gun*?"

"Yeah? So?" He asked, soon followed by a laugh. "So you really didn't believe me, huh? What do you think I do? Kill everyone with my bare hands?"

"Holy shit, Mitch," She whispered, her eyes floating around the room aimlessly.

Mitch stood, moving across the room to sit by his sister. He wrapped his arm around her shoulders, hugging her tightly.

"Myrna, I explained all of this to you already. You shouldn't be that shocked."

"I don't know what to say."

"Look, I don't always use a gun. It's not even my preferred method if you want to know the truth. I prefer a knife. But, sometimes you have to make a point. And guns make big, nasty messes. And those big nasty messes usually send a big, nasty message. This job in Reno, well, it requires a big nasty message to be sent. Besides, it'll get me in and out quicker."

He patted Myrna on the back before rising, returning to pull items from his bag. She sat watching him in shock, not knowing what to think or do. At that moment, she couldn't move. She froze in that spot, in that dirty roadside motel. Mitch looked at her, dropping his shoulders as though he was disappointed in his little sister.

"Myrna, get it together, would ya?" He said. A slight chuckle escaping his lips. "I guess the shock you're in means we can consider this payback for the little fun you pulled in the lobby. You're not so full of jokes now, are you?"

CHAPTER 19

Mitch woke to the sun beating through the motel window, slicing its way through the browning curtain that was stretched across the water spot-stained window. The soft breeze of the AC unit forced them to swing and sway just enough, and the sun had no issue cutting through the thin, cheap material to burn directly into his closed, tired eyes. He pulled his right hand from under the covers, placing it over his face so he could make sense of what was happening.

"Ugh, dammit," He muttered, lifting his body, allowing it to fall back and land upon the headboard.

He pressed his palms into his face, rubbing the sleep from his eyes, attempting to focus on something–anything–in the room. He turned to the bed opposite his to check on his sister, startled out of his morning stupor to find the bed completely empty.

"Myrna?" He asked, peering around the room. No answer. He asked again, this time louder, and with more intensity. "Myrna? Where are you?" Again, no answer.

Mitch jumped out of bed, wearing only his boxer briefs and a plain white tee. First, he rushed to the bathroom, shoving the door wide open. Empty.

"Shit," He muttered under his breath, panicking.

Exploding from the door frame, he landed hard upon his own bed. Reaching for the floor, he frantically threw his sneakers on his feet, tying them at record pace. Deep within his core, Mitch was a cold-blooded killer.

A man without a conscience. Though, with Myrna, it had always been his job to keep an eye on her, and he could never allow something to happen, especially on his watch. He needed to know where she was and he needed to know right away. Once his shoes were tied, he jumped to his feet, tearing the door open with such force, he could've torn it from the hinges. Standing in the doorway, just outside the room on the walkway was Myrna. Her eyes had been glued to the door's locking mechanism, until it jerked forward away from her. The force startled her, as she stumbled back a step or two. Her eyes, looking upward, landed into her brothers. In her hands, a plate loaded with breakfast foods.

"Bagel?" She asked, extending the plate towards him.

"Get the fuck in here," He said through gritted teeth, grabbing her by the arm.

"Whoa, calm down, dude," She shouted, stumbling into the room. "What the hell is your deal?"

"My deal?" Mitch said in fury, running his hand over the top of his head. "Where did you go? Where were you?"

"I went to get breakfast, what's the problem?"

"Don't–" He stopped himself, turning away from her. He turned back to speak. "Don't ever just disappear like that, OK? I need to know where you are at *all times*. Got it?"

"OK, first, put pants on before you yell at me like this. Highly inappropriate," She said, turning away, sitting on the end of her bed. "Second, I didn't run away. I went to get breakfast. For the *both* of us, mind you."

"I'm sorry," He finally said, sitting on the edge of the other bed. "You just scared me, that's all. It's not safe out in the world."

"Not safe? I went 40 feet away from you."

"I know, I know. I'm just, I want to know where you are. That's all. Let me know next time."

"Big brother still being protective of his helpless little sister? Aww. That's so sweet."

"Fuck you, Myrna."

"Look, this is way too much excitement this early in the morning. Let's take a deep breath and settle down. Now, do you want a bagel or a waffle?"

He remained silent for a moment, his chest heaving with deep breaths. Turning to look at her, he finally broke the silence. "Bagel."

When they finished their minimal, motel breakfasts, each of them gathered their belongings, loaded them back into the trunk and hit the road towards Reno. A short, two and a half hour drive remained between them and their next roadside motel adventure. Leaving this early in the day meant a lot more downtime inside whatever filthy room Mitch had picked out for them in the following city. And after that morning's outburst, it left Myrna nervous that she might be held captive in whatever motel room she'd find herself in later that day. Hoping to put the entire experience behind the both of them, Myrna wasted no time in connecting her phone for some tunes to accompany them on the drive.

"What are you putting on this time?" Mitch asked, checking the side mirrors. Mr. Safety driver strikes again.

"Doesn't matter," Myrna replied, snark in her tone. "I'm not taking any requests today."

"Umm, excuse me," He said, reaching for her phone.

She promptly pulled it away from him, hiding it under her right arm.

"Hey, I thought this car was a democracy. We'd vote on what gets played."

"Not a chance. You vetoed me yesterday for that old person horseshit. Today, I choose the tunes."

"Alright, alright," He gave in. "Can you at least tell me what it is?"

"Today's selection is My Chemical Romance."

"Oh, that band you wanted to go see? I remember you mentioning them."

"Yes. Now *that* would've been a cool birthday gift. Tickets to see my all-time favorite band. Especially since they haven't toured in so long."

"Sorry to disappoint you," He sniped.

"Stop, I'm only kidding. This record *The Black Parade* is amazing. Have you heard it?"

"Can't say that I have," He checked his mirrors again, changed lanes, picking up speed.

"Well, today I get to teach *you* something, Brother. What great music is. Oh, my god! I just thought of something!" She jumped in her seat, excitement building within every bone in her body.

"From your excitement I don't know if I should be happy or terrified."

"Since we're on this, whatever it is, *mission,* to kill the guy who murdered our parents. Can we call ourselves the Black Parade?"

"The *Black Parade*?" He asked, confused as he'd ever been.

"Yeah! Come on! That would be so cool! You and me. The Graves Kids. When we kill someone we can tell them 'Welcome to the Black Parade, motherfucker!' Then boom! Off with their heads. What do you say?"

"Two people can't make a parade."

"Who says?"

"I don't know, parade people? When have you seen a parade of only two people?"

"Man, you're seriously no fun," She quipped, settling into her seat disappointed. "You know what? I don't care what you say. We're the Black Parade. It's final."

"Whatever you say, Myrna."

Myrna looked out the window to see a road sign telling her, *Reno - 110 Miles.* She nodded her head, cranking the volume on the stereo. My Chemical Romance exploded from the speakers, vibrating their seats, heads and hearts.

"Prepare yourself, Reno," She said, a bright smile on her young face. "The fucking Black Parade is coming for you!"

Mitch shook his head, staring at his sister. Though, at that moment, he couldn't stop himself from smiling.

CHAPTER 20

It was just after noon when the Graves kids rolled into town, trekking through the center of Reno down Virginia Street. The sun soaked city was quiet with light car movement and minor foot traffic making up most of what they saw through the windows. No bright neon to be seen in the light of day, all the gamblers and drunks were stuck at a table hoping to win back their life savings or sleeping the day away before nightfall, preparing to do it all again under the intoxicating neon sea from above. Still, Myrna gazed in full wonderment at the tall hotels and resorts that lined the street. She'd never been to Las Vegas, Reno, or even Nevada in her life. Her only knowledge of those gambling meccas from what she'd seen on documentaries and highly suspicious pawn shop television shows. She shifted in her seat in frantic motion, pulling her cell phone from her back pocket as they approached the famous Reno arch. The desert sun sent blinding rays off the polished, silver archway, the letters proclaiming Reno as the Biggest Little City in the World. Myrna held her phone, angling it just right to capture a photo of the arch. Just before she could snap the photo, Mitch reached across the car, gently lowering her arms.

"No pictures," He whispered, shaking his head. "That's a lesson to you. No posting on social media where you are. You never know who might be keeping track of your whereabouts."

"As far as I'm aware, *you're* the only one keeping track of my whereabouts," She snarled. "Besides, I wasn't going to post anything. I wanted it for my own memories."

"Either way," He continued. "Plausible deniability is important in this business. You never want people to know where you are, or where you've been."

"Well, I've got news for you, Magellan. These phones of ours keep track of us whether we like it or not. Besides, need I remind you that your entire car is basically one, giant computer on fucking wheels?"

"Alright, alright," He said, waving her off.

"That reminds me," She chimed in, glaring at her brother. "What made you want to buy *this* car, anyway?"

"These are great cars, are you kidding me?" He scoffed. "Top of the line technology, kid. The best money can buy."

"But it has no," She sucked air through her teeth, nodding her head back and forth. "No personality. Like, this might be worse than a giant, lifted truck."

"How so?"

"I don't know. It's just like, what are you trying to prove?"

Mitch glared at her, picking up exactly what she was putting down. Keeping her focus out the front window, a smile appeared on her face, as she looked towards him from the corner of her eyes.

"Don't you worry about what message I am or am not sending with this car," He barked. "Besides, what would you drive? A Jetta?"

"No," She replied, offended. "If I had the money you clearly have, I'd drive a vintage hearse."

"Oh my god, Myrna. You're such a cliche."

"Fuck off. A hearse would be fun to drive. And it says something."

"Oh yeah? What? You prefer spending time with the dead over the living?"

"If that's the statement, it would actually be the perfect car for you, now wouldn't it?"

Again, Mitch glared at his sister, sending daggers from his eyes to hers. He didn't want to spend his time with the dead. Of course he didn't. He only wanted to profit from the dead. Nevertheless, he understood her point.

"What glorious motel do you have us staying in this time? Extended Stay Homicide? Motel 666 with an elevator straight to hell? Or hey, why not make it easy on everyone, huh? Let's just spend the night in the morgue."

"Myrna, we've talked about this. Once we handle business, I'll take you to stay in the nicest hotel you've ever seen. I promise you. But while we do business, we need to do things my way. There's a reason they haven't caught me."

"Yet," She said with an eyebrow raised.

"Really nice, kid. You want your brother to go away forever? You want me gone?"

"No, of course not. I'm sorry. I'll let up. I swear."

"Don't worry about where we're staying. Besides, we need to make a stop first. I have a surprise for you."

Mitch turned right on California Avenue, pulling over to park against the curb only a few blocks up. He had stopped in front of a storefront for Sharpshooter's Boutique. A one-story brick building painted beige, with large glass windows in front allowing foot traffic to see inside. They'd covered the windows with hand-painted designs of six shooters and banners displaying the store's name.

"A *gun* store?" Myrna blurted. "Are you serious right now?"

"I'm buying you a present."

"I don't want a gun, Mitch."

"Good," Mitch said through a smile, opening the driver side door. "Because I'm not buying you one."

Myrna shook her head, reluctantly exiting the car. They stood side by side looking up at the storefront. The Reno sun beat down upon them, the dry heat burning into their skin as they stood. Mitch placed his right hand on Myrna's back, ushering her towards the front door. When he opened it to allow Myrna to enter, a bell on a string clacked back and forth, smacking into the pane of glass alerting the clerk that customers had arrived. The room stunk of old wood, metal polish and stale carpet. To the left, behind the counter, were many racks of different rifles and other firearms. The center, filled with multiple racks displaying hunting clothes, different camo items and gear. The counter itself was a glass display showcasing different knives, scopes and other gear Myrna had never seen before.

"Good Afternoon," The man behind the counter said. He held a wooden rifle, sat on the counter by the stock, rubbing it with a stained, yellow towel. "How can I help y'all today?"

"We're looking for a good knife," Mitch said, the smile still on his face. He placed his hand on Myrna's shoulder. "My sister's *first* knife, that is."

"Ahh," The man replied. His face towards the ceiling, his eyes closed as he fantasized about something.

Myrna didn't want to know what that something was.

"We all remember our first, don't we," He continued.

Mitch laughed at the comment. Myrna, thinking she couldn't feel any more uncomfortable, found a new level of yuck. The man sniffed the air, taking in a deep breath before returning his attention to the two customers.

"Well, lucky you. We have plenty to choose from. Step right on up and take a look. Let me know if you want to check something out."

Mitch pushed Myrna slightly to get her feet moving, the discomfort taking over her body, making the ability for voluntary movement difficult. They approached the case, looking over the wide array of knives and other objects inside. Myrna allowed her fingertips to tickle the top of the case, the lights from within struck her, creating bright bulbs inside her eyes.

"See anything you like?" Mitch asked, peering into the case.

She scanned the knives on display, remaining silent, until she found one that was to her liking.

"How about this one, right here?" She asked, her finger pressed into the glass over a specific blade.

The knife she chose looked like some sort of medieval dagger. Its blade curved slightly, the handle made of steel that intertwined creating an almost Celtic look. The end of the handle adorned with a large dragon's head with fake gems for eyes.

"Come on, Myrna. Get real. Your knife won't be for display or some sort of cosplay. This is a knife that should and *will* be used."

"What? I like that one. Isn't this supposed to be my gift? My choice?"

"Well, yeah. But, you need one you can actually use. Trust me, that's not going to do what you want it to. It's all for show. No offense," Mitch held a hand towards the clerk.

"None taken. You're not wrong. We get plenty of local kids, much like you, ma'am, who love that kind of play around shit."

"Fine, whatever," Myrna said, shaking them both off. She scanned the case some more. "OK, how about this one right here?"

The knife in question this go around was a more typical looking tool. A long, 6.5 inch blade with a leather handle, a silver cross pressed deep into the material. Enough to get the job done, and yet, just goth enough to make her happy.

"Now that's a knife," Mitch said proudly. "Can we see it?"

The clerk pulled the knife from the case, handing it slowly and carefully to Myrna. She held it in her hands in awe of its weight. The comfort of the handle shocked her, as well as the ease at which she could move it.

"What do you think?" Mitch asked.

"I actually like it. I *really* like it."

"Looks like we've got a winner. We'll take it."

The clerk placed the knife in a sheath, promptly placing it into a paper bag, the top crumpled over. Mitch dropped cash onto the glass display, and they were off. On the drive to their next home away from home for the evening, Myrna held the bag in her lap, a smile that wouldn't leave her face which was clear to her proud brother. She didn't say a word until they arrived. Even when they entered the parking lot to the Lucky Strike Motel, its sign boasting it as The Biggest Little Motel in the World, she kept any comments she otherwise would've had to herself. Mitch quickly checked in at the front desk, Myrna waiting outside the 3-story, white and red trimmed motel. She held the bag with both hands close to her body, gazing towards the horizon wondering what the future held for her and her new, trusty friend. And the possibilities made her giddy.

CHAPTER 21

The room at the Lucky Strike was wildly familiar to the motel they had stayed in the night before. The designers had positioned two strikingly similar beds in the exact spots. Same shitty, deteriorating nightstand with an eerily similar lamp and phone between them. One short, wooden dresser with a flat panel television set on top, even the bathroom seemed to be in the same area of the room. Almost as though the same planner and designers had worked in both Reno and Sacramento. Although, it could be absolutely factual. Most cheap motels look identical on the inside. Completely unremarkable and indistinguishable from one another once you're in the room.

Myrna sat on the edge of the bed, her knife in her lap. She continued to admire it, picking it up every so often to, as Mitch instructed her, to get used to the weight of the thing. Handle in hand, she held it so she could stab outward, then with the blade down as though she was striking something below her. Playing with a deadly weapon wasn't only encouraged, it was actually a necessity. Mitch sat at the terrible coffee table next to the window, taking apart his pistol.

"Do you need to have that gun out every time we step foot in a room?" She asked, setting the knife onto her thighs.

"This is my instrument," He said, holding the revolver into the air. "And I firmly believe in keeping my instrument finely tuned."

He set the gun down, putting an old rag to a tin canister, tipping it sideways allowing whatever liquid was inside to soak through. He polished and cleaned the components of the pistol, looking over his work before continuing. Again, Myrna's eyes couldn't break away from the gold lettering on the side of the pistol. Those letters, A and L, shimmering like a beacon in the dimly lit room.

"What do those letters mean?" She finally asked.

"Hmm?" Mitch looked at her, confused. At first, he didn't know what she was referring to.

"Those gold letters? A and L? AL? What's that mean?"

Mitch held the pistol, turning it slightly in his right hand, admiring the finish of the thing.

"Oh, that," He said, continuing to wipe it down. "Something from the manufacturer, I guess? I'd never really thought about it. How does that knife feel in your hands?"

"Feels good," Myrna allowed the conversation to shift.

"Yeah? You feeling comfortable with it? Can you get the job done? And you're sure you know how to handle that thing? You're comfortable with it?"

"I mean, yeah," She scoffed. "It's a knife. How hard could it be?"

"It's not that easy, Myrna. You need to not only understand your enemy, you also need to fully understand your instrument."

Myrna held the knife, rocking it back and forth in her palm. She watched as the minimal light from the fading bulb in the cheap lamp reflected off its clean blade.

"Myrna, you look confused. You can't be confused when you're thrown into a live situation."

"Come on, man," She said, dropping the knife hard onto the bed. "I don't know what you want from me. This is what you do, apparently. It's all new and foreign to me. Cut me some slack."

"Alright," He said, letting out a deep breath as he rose. "Let me show you a couple of things, OK? Hand me the knife."

Mitch held it inside his palm, spinning and maneuvering it around his body, checking the weight. Getting familiar with the feel of the deadly weapon. Holding it to his face, he admired the sharpness, flicking his finger tip at the sharp side of the blade.

"OK, now pay attention. This shit is very important. Stand up for a moment."

Myrna stood, following her brother to the end of both beds. More room for instruction. More room for playtime.

"Do you know where to stab someone to kill them?"

She pushed her index finger into the direct center of his chest with an exaggerated, nervous smile.

"That's one way. Check this out," He said. He put the tip of the knife against the left side of her chest. "This right here? That's the heart. That is a good hit and is absolutely fatal. Once you drive a blade into someone's heart, they may squirm and scream, but it won't take long for them to expire."

"OK, so, strike the heart. Got it."

"Well, that's not the only place," He said, his eyes filled with pure excitement. Clearly, he loved discussing this topic. One of his favorites, she could tell. He pressed the sharp side of the blade lightly against his sister's throat. "There's always the throat, right? You should already know that. From all those dumb movies you're obsessed with. Now, you can either stab someone directly through the throat, or you can *slash* their throat. If you go this route, make sure you really dig the blade into their flesh, OK? Don't pussy foot it. You go deep enough into the throat and there's no way they come back from that shit. This is also a fatal hit."

He held the handle with the blade pointing downwards, letting the tip of the knife barely tickle the top of her head.

"You can always stab someone right in the head. The zombie kill, I like to call it. But then you're fighting with some serious bone. To do this, you really need to put some muscle into it."

He knelt before her, pressing the sharp side into her upper thigh.

"And if you really want to punish someone, you can slash right here, against their inner thigh. That's messy as shit because they'll bleed out, and I mean bleed *everywhere*. That strike will require quite a bit of cleanup, but it's absolutely fatal. Got it?"

He stood, spun the knife in his hand, passing it handle side back to Myrna. She continued admiring the blade, twisting the handle in her hand.

"How do you know all of this? You learned it as you went along?"

Mitch remained silent for a moment, his eyes locked onto Myrna's. The look in his eyes told a story–an unpleasant one. His breath heaved in and out as he glared, the look on his face saying a million words at once, each one indecipherable to Myrna. A nervousness grew within her soul as he glared down towards her.

"A friend," He finally said under his breath. "A long time ago. An old friend."

Mitch turned, returning to the seat at the coffee table. He hurried and put the pistol pieces back into place, shoving it into his duffle bag. Standing, he stretched his lower back before laying on his respective bed, his right arm stretched across his face.

"I have a long night ahead of me. I need to get some rest."

"What should I do?"

"I don't care," He barked. "Just keep it down and let me rest. I need to be sharp tonight."

CHAPTER 22

Mitch woke to golden rays that poured through the window, just barely lighting the room. Golden hour was upon them. He knew the day had passed and it was almost showtime. A big 40k payout on the other end of a few bad guys he'd never met, had nothing against, but, more than anything in his life, wanted them dead. The room remained absolutely silent aside from the rustling of his own sheets.

"Mother fucker," He muttered, rubbing his eyes.

Myrna had taken off–again. He thought he made it abundantly clear he wanted to know where she was at all times, and yet again he found himself alone in another cheap, shady motel room. Slowly he pulled himself from the bed and dressed himself for the long night that awaited him. A few minutes later he emerged from the motel room wearing a pair of athletic warm-up pants, a plain black tee and all black sneakers. As the door shut behind him, across the parking lot he noticed the pool area. It wasn't much to speak of, nothing more than a typical motel pool surrounded by a tall, black iron gate. Stretched out in a lounge chair was Myrna, her face buried deep into a paperback. Crossing the parking lot, he pulled open the gate, entering the pool area. His nose stung immediately from the overuse of pool chemicals that drifted through the air. A couple of teenage boys splashed together, making a mess sending water all over, drenching anything within their own personal splash zone. Their flailing movements sent water flying every which way as they played an intense game of grab ass with one another.

He kept his protective eyes on them as he moved towards Myrna, knowing full well their antics were indeed their own attempt, as pathetic as it may be, to get the older girl's attention. Myrna's jet black hair had been pulled into a tight ponytail, her bangs combed neatly over her forehead. She wore a cutoff, black tee, the logo of some punk band Mitch had never heard of wearing away on the front. A pair of her signature black cut off jean shorts on her body, though the button was undone and she'd pulled them a bit too low for Mitch's liking. She wore a pair of pitch black sunglasses as she read her book.

"What did I tell you about sneaking off?"

"I didn't sneak off," She said in a low, annoyed tone, not looking away from her book. "I wanted to read and this felt like a nice place to do so."

"Yeah, OK," He said, scanning the surrounding area. "You know these boys are watching you? Looking at you?"

"So? What do I care? Let them look."

"I don't like it."

"Then why don't you tell *them* that? Don't bother me with that information. Just because a couple of pervy teenagers can't keep their eyes in their skull doesn't mean I need to be put in a prison."

"Right," He replied with a deep sigh. "Look, I need to head out. I have work to do. We can get outta here as soon as I'm finished."

"What's in the bag?"

"Don't worry about it."

Myrna dropped the paperback onto her right thigh, lowering her sunglasses, peering up at her brother.

"You wanna drop the whole tough guy routine with me? I'm your sister, not your associate."

"You're right. I'm sorry. It's the tools of the trade. Rather not discuss in the open."

"Right," She said with a smirk and a giggle.

"I won't be back until late. Will you be OK here by yourself? You know I can't risk bringing you along."

"I think I'll be fine, Brother," She returned her sunglasses, lifting the novel.

"Don't go running off around town, OK? We'll rendezvous when things are clear. And tomorrow, we're on our way to Eureka."

"Can't wait," She said, full attitude on display, thumbing to the next page in her book.

Mitch turned to leave the pool when Myrna called for his attention.

"Mitch. Please, whatever it is you're doing tonight. Be safe, OK? I really wouldn't be able to handle something happening to you."

"Don't worry, kid. I'm always safe. I love you, Myrna."

She kissed her palm, blew into it in his direction. When he smiled, she shrugged her shoulders with a coy smile. Pulling open the gate to leave, he allowed it to slam shut behind him.

***

Hours later, the door to the motel room burst open with enough force it crashed into the drywall behind, leaving a small yet obvious indentation where the knob had struck. Startled from slumber, Myrna bounced, sitting up on the bed, her hands pressed into the mattress behind her. The room was pitch black, illuminated now only by dim light coming from the outside street lamps as they flooded through the wide open doorway.

"What the *fuck!?*" She screamed. "Who is it? Who's there?"

A figure stood in the shadows of the room looming over her. The figure grabbed the door, slamming it shut with so much force, it rattled the walls of the room.

"Pack your shit," A gravel filled voice said. "We've got to get out of here."

"What the fuck is going on!?"

The shadow figure flicked the light switch, the dull lamp coming to life lighting the room. Standing by the coffee table was Mitch, blood splatter covering most of his body. His bare arms, his face, neck and hair dripped, like he'd run through a blood sprinkler.

"Oh my god, Mitch! What the fuck happened? Are you OK?"

"I'll explain later. Just pack your shit. *Now!*"

As Mitch grabbed any items he'd left behind, tossing them into his bag, Myrna jumped from bed as though lightning had struck her in the ass. As quick as her body would allow, she threw every item she could get her trembling hands on into her backpack.

"Can you at least tell me if you're OK?" She asked, her voice shaking. "You look hurt!"

"I'll be fine," He promised. "Just pack and get to the car."

Throwing his duffel bag over his right shoulder, he pulled the door open. With his left hand, he ushered Myrna out as she stumbled through the doorway onto the cold cement. With her backpack thrown over her shoulder, she held a pair of torn up Vans sneakers in her right hand. Mitch clicked the key fob unlocking the doors. They jumped into the car as Mitch tore out of the parking lot, the wheels skidding along the pavement as he did so. Pushing through a red light, he turned left onto Virginia Street. Myrna watched through the windshield as he sped underneath the famous Reno arch, peeling out and turning onto the 80 freeway heading East.

"*What the fuck is going on!?*" Myrna screamed, her hands open wide, trembling next to her head as she screamed.

"Lower your voice, for God's sake," Mitch shouted, his eyes closed, his right hand pressed against his temple. "Please. My head is splitting wide open."

"Mitch, please tell me what the hell happened. You're covered in blood."

"It's not mine," He whispered, inspecting his arms. "Well, most of it isn't at least."

"Oh my god," Myrna whispered, falling against the passenger door, her eyes locked onto her brother. "You really are a killer, aren't you?"

"Wait, you still didn't believe me?"

"I, I," She stuttered, trying to find the right words to say. "I really didn't know. Being told your brother is a killer is like trying to eat day-old shrimp. It's pretty hard to fucking digest, don't you think?"

"Well, start digesting, kid. It's true."

"Holy shit," She whispered to herself. "What happened? Did you get the money?"

"Look in the back seat," He nodded his head towards the back.

Myrna pulled her body forward, leaning between the front seats. In the back was a brown, leather briefcase. She settled back into her chair, a look of immediate shock covering her young face. Her bottom lip quivered as it hung wide open.

"Believe me, now?"

She looked back at her brother, her mouth still wide open in shock.

"Are you going to tell me what happened?" She asked calmly. As calmly as she could.

"Don't worry, I'll give you all the grisly details later. I need to make a call first. All part of the job."

Mitch pulled his phone from his pants, dialing and pressing it to the right side of his face. Myrna could hear clear as day what was happening on the other end of the phone. One ring, followed by a deep, accented voice on the other line. No hello, no pleasantries. The mysterious voice on the other end was all business.

"*Is it done?*" The voice asked.

"Yeah," Mitch confirmed with a sigh. "We're all set. It's handled. Leaving town, now."

"*Good.*"

"Talk to you soon," Mitch said. Before Mitch could hang up, the voice beckoned back to him.

"*What about our second job? Is this handled yet or not?*"

Mitch looked across the car towards his sister, her eyes trained on him like a homing missile locked onto a target.

"Not quite. But it'll be done soon."

"*Good. Don't let me down.*" The call ended abruptly.

Mitch dropped the phone into the center console, running his right hand over his head. He let out a series of deep breaths, looking at his blood-soaked hands and arms.

CHAPTER 23

Mitch kept the gas pedal pressed firmly into the floorboards, the engine of his electric vehicle screaming up the 395 out of Reno. For the first few miles, Myrna's body wouldn't allow her to sit back in her seat, her knuckles white from grasping the grab handle, her body pulled forward. After his phone call, Mitch went silent. His movements were jerky, frantic. His eyes remained wide open, wild, and she wasn't sure if he'd even blinked since starting the drive. She had stopped trying to reason with her brother to drive more carefully, as for the first few miles he wouldn't even respond to the words as she shrieked and screamed. By mile 10, she'd had enough of his lack of response and reckless driving. Speeding down the freeway, switching lanes at breakneck speeds, passing by early morning drivers, semi-trucks and anything else in their way.

"*Mitch!*" She screamed, her body again being tossed into the door as he side swept another big rig. "God dammit, Mitch! *Listen to me!* You need to slow the fuck down!"

"Not until we get out of Nevada," He whispered to himself. "Have to get out of Nevada. Someone could be following us. Need to get out of Nevada."

Typically, someone doused head to toe in other people's blood might choose to drive rather reasonably. Though, at this moment Mitch was an unreasonable man. The thought nor idea of being pulled over by police hadn't crossed his mind, clearly, he feared something far worse. The types of men Mitch kept in his company were much more terrifying than local, hillbilly cops in the middle of nothingness. To these men, there was no rule of law. There was no ability to plead your case. Absolutely no presumption of innocence with these folks. If you were seen as guilty, that was it. The stamp of death was on your back. A stamp that no amount of scrubbing would leave your skin. So he drove and he drove fast.

They stormed through Border Town, a tiny place that was just as it sounds; a small roadside stop sitting on the border between California and Nevada. Surrounded by vast, empty space, it was the last stop on the way out of Nevada to fill up on gas, pick up food or maybe place a bet or two at its modest casino. Once the *Welcome to California* sign came into view, Myrna felt the engine calm, their speed slowing considerably. Merging across all lanes of the freeway, Mitch took the very next off ramp for Long Valley Road, comfortably cruising through a stop sign at the end of the exit, continuing down the frontage road that ran alongside the empty desert.

"What are you doing? Where are we going?" Myrna asked, sitting forward in her seat. She couldn't stop the tremors overtaking her body.

"There's a campsite up the road a bit," Mitch said, letting out a deep, relaxing breath. "I can't keep traveling while looking like this. Anyone sees me and I'm toast. They'll have a shower I can sneak into no problem. I need to clean myself up and we both need to get some rest before we keep going."

"Mitch," Myrna stopped herself, turning to stare out the window. Her eyes, glassy as they filled with tears. Shaking her head, she turned to look at her brother. "What the hell happened back there?"

"It's all part of the job, Myrna," He said through a sigh, annoyed at the question. "All in a day's work."

On the left side of the road was the entrance to the Happy Camper RV Park. A wooden sign showing severe decay from years of sun bleaching and deterioration was hand carved with a smiling family standing outside an RV. Their hands up in a wave, as though welcoming any road weary travelers to stop in and take a load off. The entrance was equipped with a small booth surrounded by glass windows where at a normal time of day, a park ranger or towny employee might grant access to travelers and campers. Now, as the sun was just beginning to sneak its way over the mountains, the booth remained unmanned, making it a cinch to drive around the lowered, mechanical arm and access the campgrounds facilities.

For the most part, the campground appeared to be empty, summer travelers not arriving yet on their way through the pass. Mitch drove deep through the grounds until they came across a small building tucked back behind some of the modest campsites. The building with its sun bleached tiles that were caked in desert sand and dust covered a stucco hut with no doors or windows. Equipped with two wide-open entrances, one on either side, to enter the bathroom facilities. Carefully, Mitch pulled the car through a campsite next to the building before shutting off the engine.

"Do you need to shower or anything? Use the bathroom? This would be a good place to do it. No one around."

"I have nothing to hide from," Myrna said, her facial expression showing pure confusion. "And no, I'm not going to shower here. Mitch, tell me what happened to you. You're covered in someone else's body fluid. I don't even know how to talk to you. To be quite honest, I'm terrified of you right now."

"You don't have anything to be afraid of," He said, acting completely dismissive. "We needed to get out of there, that's all. We're safe here. For now."

"*For now?* Wow, that is really reassuring."

"What do you want me to tell you, Myrna? This is my life, OK? This is what I do. It's not the first time and trust me, it won't be the last."

"I just want to know what the hell happened. Why we had to leave in such a hurry? Why it felt like we were running for our lives back there. I'm in this with you now. I think I have every right to know–"

"OK, OK!" He cut in, covering his ears with his blood-soaked palms. "Fine, you want to know what happened? I'll tell you what happened."

"That is all I'm asking."

"You want the details?" He asked. "Settle in. I'll tell you everything."

CHAPTER 24

The Night Before...

A colossal, Spanish-style home sat at the far end of a long road. Daytime life had retired for the day hours ago, allowing the nighttime creatures to come out and play. The lack of streetlights on the quiet, lonesome street allowed for all kinds of unsavory things to occur under the blanket of night. None of the homes on this quiet road were too close to one another for privacy's sake, of course. While the other homes had turned their lights down hours prior, one particular house at the end of the block was still alive and well, its windows illuminated from within. Though the light was minimal to watchers from the streets, thanks to being covered by thick, expensive shades. No peering eyes were welcome to look upon the activity within this home while the mice scurried about inside. A driveway paved with expensive Spanish tile led to the massive home's three-car garage, the doors appearing like something stolen off a castle from a faraway land. The stucco on the outside was pristine, its large windows stretching high into the air. Between two square stucco areas of the home, smack dab in the middle sat a brick spire.

The main room of the home had a sunken living room with two hardwood steps built all the way around. Wrapping the sunken space were expensive, beige sofas with a wide, antique, hand carved table in the middle of the room. To the right of the sunken living room area was an open concept kitchen with beautifully tiled floors, marble countertops and stainless steel appliances. Just past the living area, a spiral staircase led inhabitants and guests upstairs. Everything within the home as far as you could see was expensive. From the framed, original art on the walls, to the vases filled with fresh-cut flowers. Even the random tchotchkes that decorated shelves all around looked expensive, elegant and foreign. Like a well-curated museum display.

Four men, each dressed in freshly pressed, tailored suits sat upon the beige couches. On the table, an open duffle bag. Inside, bricks of white powder wrapped in cellophane taped shut with silver duct tape.

"So, are we going to get this transaction under way? Or are we going to sit with our thumbs up our asses and talk about the weather?" One man said, unbuttoning his dark blue suit jacket. His slicked black hair was seasoned with just the right amount of salt and pepper on the sides above his ears.

"Patience, patience," Another man said with a laugh. He wore a beige suit that was lost into a blob of color as he sat upon the pricey sofa. "Antonio, do the honors, huh?"

The man to his right wore a dark gray suit and sported a thin mustache above his lip. Throwing the right side of his jacket open, he retrieved a long knife from his belt, pulling one brick from the bag. As he held the brick in his hand, he sliced through the cellophane with a smile plastered across his face. He dropped the brick from where he stood, allowing it to crash upon the wooden, antique table. The drop forced the tiniest cloud of white powder to poof into the air.

"There you go, Mr. Fucking Impatient," He said, sheathing his knife, taking a seat.

The fourth man in the room sat uncomfortably quiet on the edge of the couch, a brown, leather briefcase on the floor close to his leather shoes. He had a curly mop of hair and what could be described as an 8 o'clock shadow over his face. He wore thick, black-rimmed glasses and shuffled nervously, watching but staying quiet.

"Mr. Fucking Impatient, huh?" The man in blue said, sitting forward. "You're lucky we're doing business, tough guy. I don't even let my wife talk to me like that."

"Just check the merchandise, would you?" Dark Gray said, shaking his head.

Dark Blue leaned forward, staring at the other two men through the tops of his eyes, unamused. When he felt comfortable enough to break his burning stare, he pulled a knife of his own from the inside of his jacket. Pressing a button, the blade shot out with an audible snap. He dipped the knife into the brick of powder, bringing the blade to his nose. A quick sniff through his right nostril, he tilted his head back, tapping on his throat.

"Now," He spoke, clearing his throat. "You wouldn't be trying to sell me on some baby powder mixed bullshit wrapped as pure Columbian, would you?"

"What the fuck are you implying?" Dark Gray barked, sitting forward.

Beige suit extended his right arm, shaking his head. It was enough to get Dark Gray to sit back, relax. Beige was clearly calling the shots for Dark Gray, and he wanted Dark Gray to pipe down.

"My guy here doesn't mean any disrespect, please excuse him," Beige said in a calm tone. "And I assure you, this is as good as you're going to get on this side of any border, my friend."

"Hmm," Dark Blue nodded his head. "And how much of this have you got to accompany that little baggy of yours?"

"Plenty," Dark Gray shouted, his aggression on full display.

"Please. Let the adults speak," Beige said, burning a hole through Dark Gray with his intense eyes.

"Fine," Dark Gray said, patting his thighs. "I'm gonna go take a piss anyway."

"Oh, uh, yeah," Curly Hair stuttered. "It's, uh. It's down the hall."

"Down the hall? Gimme a fucking break. I'll piss outside. Besides, I need to smoke, too."

Dark Gray made his way through the kitchen, opening the double glass doors that led to a perfectly manicured backyard. Beautiful palm trees and flowers surrounded a large pond outback, set amongst the greenest grass one had ever seen. He opened his jacket, removing a pack of cigarettes. Pulling one from the pack, he flicked a lighter, exhaling a plume of smoke into the night air. Dark Gray moved towards the pond, unzipping his suit pants. As he relieved himself into the pond water, he exhaled another plume of white clouds from his lips, accompanied by a soft laugh.

"Fuck this pond. Stupid tough guy, bitch," He muttered, the cigarette dangling from his lips.

The sound of urine splashing the pond water distracted him just enough not to notice the footsteps that moved towards him from behind. An arm from the darkness then grabbed Dark Gray, wrapping around across his chest. Before he could make even the slightest of sound, a sharp blade dug into the flesh of his neck. The blade sliced deeper and deeper as he slashed. Dark Gray felt a hand grab his hair, pulling his head backwards as he gurgled and squirmed, warm, copper liquid pouring from the gaping wound in his neck down his chest and splashing into the pond. The slash was so deep and wide across his neck, it almost snapped his head clean off. Soon, Dark Gray's legs gave out as he toppled forward into the pond creating a loud splash.

Standing in his place was Mitch, dressed in black, short-sleeved work coveralls. A rag hung from the belt area, which he promptly used to wipe the blood from his blade. He turned, looking into the home through the back, glass doors. He knew that splash was no good and could cause some serious trouble. Through the glass, he saw all three men stand from the sofa.

"Shit," He muttered, turning to run towards the opposite end of the house.

"What the fuck was that?" Dark Blue shouted, standing, pulling a pistol from his jacket. "Who the fuck is here?"

"I, I don't know, sir. I swear," Curly Hair shouted, his hands in front of his body to keep these maniacs at bay.

Beige Suit stood, also brandishing a pistol from his jacket.

"We've got a *rat* in our midst," He looked at Dark Blue. "Is he one of *yours?* Huh?"

"I'll let that one insult slide," Dark Blue said, pointing the gun at Beige. "Next time, I'm burying a bullet between those eyes of yours. Got it?"

"Who is he?" Beige asked Curly Hair.

"I told you, I don't know!"

"Come on," Beige shouted at Dark Blue. "We've got to kill this piece of shit before he ruins this transaction for the both of us."

Beige and Dark Blue rushed through the back doors, turning immediately to their left. Mitch darted towards the end of the home, diving through an open window. *BOOM! BOOM! BOOM!* Shots rang out, echoing throughout the landscape.

"He's inside," Dark Blue said. "He's got to be going for that bag! Stay here, wait him out. A rat will always surface when shit gets desperate."

Both men stood on the back patio, their pistols drawn through the open doorway. Everything was silent, the only noise to be heard, the loud breathing from the nervous men as they waited for a mystery person to appear before them. From an upstairs window, one single shot rang out like a thunderclap from the heavens. Dark Blue recoiled as it struck him in the right shoulder. He screamed in absolute pain as he fell to one knee, quickly regaining his composure and standing to his feet.

"The motherfucker is upstairs. Fucking *get him!*"

Like a lightning strike, Beige rushed inside, followed slowly by Dark Blue, clutching his right shoulder and staggering as he moved. Blood trickled through his fingers, covering the entirety of his suit jacket. Beige Suit ran for the stairs, taking them two at a time.

"If this scumbag works with you, I'll feed you to my dogs, you hear me?" Dark Blue screamed, pointing his pistol at Curly Hair's face.

Upstairs, Mitch holstered his pistol behind his back and made for the door. Just as his hand reached for the handle, shots burst through the wood, splintering it, sending shards all over. Mitch, covering his ears, dove across the room, landing hard onto his stomach. When his body hit the ground, he had knocked the wind out of himself. Just as he rolled to his back he saw what was left of the door being kicked in. Beige Suit entered like a professional wrestler, chest puffed, ready to attack. When he looked to his right, he saw Mitch, splayed across the carpet. Lifting his pistol, he tightened his grip trying to squeeze the trigger. Before he could pop off a shot, Mitch lifted his right leg, cocked it back then with any strength he could find, burst his foot forwards, kicking Beige Suit in the kneecap. His knee folded back in the wrong direction, turning his right leg into a V shape. As he fell in pain, the gun lifted into the air, the shot crashing into the drywall, missing Mitch all together.

Mitch jumped to his feet, heaving and trying the best he could to catch his breath. When he looked towards the man, Beige Suit lifted his pistol yet again. He slapped the pistol away with his left hand, landing a stiff blow to Beige Suit's chin. Beige Suit fell, landing on his back as Mitch mounted him. He tore a knife from a holster driving it deep into Beige Suit's chest, pulverizing flesh, tissue and muscle on its way to his heart. Beige Suit gritted his teeth, as blood gurgled up his throat, showcasing a mouth full of deep, crimson liquid that now stained his teeth.

"You'll never get away with this, you sick fuck," Beige Suit grunted, blood boiling over his quivering lips, dripping down his cheeks. "Our bosses will *gut* you for this."

"Is that so?" Mitch asked, pulling the knife from his chest. "You mean, like *this*?"

Jumping to his feet, Mitch dug the blade deep into the man's abdomen, just below his ribcage. Tearing and sawing downward, Mitch cut him wide open from ribs to pelvis, exposing his insides to the outside.

"Tell him I'll be waiting for him," Mitch said, tearing the knife from his body. He wiped his face with the back of his hand, still working to catch his breath.

When Mitch moved to the destroyed door frame, he peaked around to the hall before looking down to the first floor of the home. He caught a quick glance of Dark Blue, his gun trained on the doorway. Mitch ducked inside just as a shot rang out, the bullet crushing through the drywall and wood, sending a plume of dust into the air.

"Come on out, you rat bastard, you! You'll never get away with this!"

Dark Blue looked towards Curly Hair, to the briefcase by his feet, to the bag of bricks on the table, then to the front door.

"Fuck it all," He screamed.

Dark Blue raced into the sunken living room, grabbed the duffle bag by the straps, then jumped over the table knocking Curly Hair to the couch. He snatched the briefcase, picking up speed and making for the front door.

"No!" Curly Hair screamed, reaching for the case that was just out of his grasp. "Not the case! Not the case!"

"Shit," Mitch muttered to himself, still pressed against the wall of the upstairs room.

Mitch emerged into the hallway bolting towards the staircase, reaching for the pistol at his back. In one motion, he jumped from the top of the spiral staircase, plummeting towards the first floor. As he fell through the air, he fired shot after shot towards Dark Blue. Most of the bullets struck the front door, though he got lucky with one striking him in the back of his right leg. Dark Blue fell to the ground mere feet from escape. Only a few feet from getting away from the violence with both the duffle bag and suitcase.

Breaking Mitch's fall was a desk that sat butted up against the wall just underneath the spiral staircase. His body crashed through the vintage desk, debris flung across the room in all directions. Rolling around in pain from the crash and fall, he tried to pull himself to his feet. Before he could gain his footing, he was tackled to the hardwood floor. Dark Blue, pumped full of adrenaline and the will to live, sat upon his chest, his trembling, bloody hands wrapped around Mitch's throat. He squeezed and squeezed, Mitch trying with all of his strength to fight him off. To somehow survive this terrible turn of events.

"We told you that you'd never get away with this, you piece of *shit!*" Dark Blue screamed, hate dripping from every pore, pressing harder and harder, as Mitch began to lose vision.

Dark Blue let go with his right hand, pulling a knife from inside his jacket. With a click, the blade flashed before Mitch's eyes. Wrapping his hands around Dark Blue's wrist, he fought with what he had left in him, as the blade inched closer and closer just above his left eyeball.

"Mitch, watch out!" Curly Hair shouted from across the room.

A single shot then rang through the home. As Mitch turned his head to the right, Dark Blue's blade sliced the flesh on his cheek. The bullet had ripped through Dark Blue's body, straight through the middle of his chest. Dropping the knife to the hardwood, he lost grip on Mitch's throat. Mitch gasped for air to fill his lungs, as Dark Blue fell onto his back next to Mitch, writhing and squirming in pain. Mitch slowly regained his composure, pulling himself to his feet. Without saying a single word, Mitch positioned himself behind Dark Blue, grabbing him by the hair and lifting his head from the floor. Reaching behind his back, he pulled the blade from its holster and dug it deeper and deeper into Dark Blue's neck, sawing and hacking as he fell into pure madness. He pulled back on Dark Blue's hair, twisting and snapping to the right. Dark Blue's head now turned in the wrong direction, facing behind him. Mitch settled onto his knees, covered head to toe in blood from the vicious scene. Curly Hair ran to him, kneeling to his right side.

"Mitch, are you OK? My God, I've never seen you take a beating like this before. Why the hell did you make that jump?"

With his mouth hanging wide open, he sucked air frantically. He grabbed Curly Hair by the collar, pulling him in close.

"Help me up, Morris," Mitch whispered, cringing as he stood. "You know I've always wanted to be an action hero. Why not start now?"

Morris, grabbing Mitch from under the arms, helped him to his feet. Mitch knelt down, his hands pressed firmly into his thighs. Once he had caught his breath, he stood upright. He held the knife towards Morris, who kept his hands in front of his body to create distance between himself and this killer.

"Tell me there aren't any more of them, Morris. Please."

"This was it, it was just the four of us. I swear."

Mitch slunk towards the front door.

"Mitch, I thought it was supposed to be two of you on this job?"

"Nope, just me," Mitch said through whispers.

"But, the boss. He told me to expect two of you. 20 grand each if you'd kill these fuckers so we could intercept the shipment they have coming in through town."

"Well, Morris, you got me, OK?" Mitch held his hands outward with a slight bow. "Now, I'll take my 40 grand, thank you very much."

"But it was supposed to be 20 *each*."

Mitch stopped, stood up straight, pulled his pistol from the holster on his back, pointing it at Morris.

"Two guys, 20 grand each. You got one guy, *me*. And I finished the job, didn't I? Now you can have your guys intercept the shipment, and I'm leaving town with my 40 grand. Don't worry, I'll let the boss know what he needs to know."

When he reached the front door, he lifted the brown suitcase, flicking the locks to look inside. Folded and wrapped inside was 40 grand in crisp bills.

"Beautiful," Mitch whispered to himself.

After he opened the front door to leave, Morris called to him as he stepped into the fresh, cool early morning air.

"Mitch. Out of curiosity. Where is the other guy?"

Mitch stopped dead in his tracks, turning just his head to look over his left shoulder. An angry scowl wrapped his blood-soaked face.

"What does it matter?" He asked, his tone serious. "The job is done, isn't it?"

CHAPTER 25

It may have been the fact that he finally filled her in on the details of the work and what had happened a few hours before and knowing, through it all, he was alive and well. Or it could've been the fresh, morning air of the desert breezing and swooshing over her exposed skin, but Myrna felt an odd sense of relaxation wash over her. For the first time in the last few days, she felt a sense of calm within her spirit. While her brother had disappeared into the restroom to scrub the death from his skin, Myrna rested her bones at a picnic table placed firmly in the sand. She basked in the morning sun in a white New York Dolls tee, the sleeves rolled to her shoulders and tucked into her black cut-off jean shorts. Her hair was tied up out of her face, her dark sunglasses protecting her eyes from the intense morning sunshine. While waiting for Mitch, she flipped through a tattered horror paperback she'd found at the bottom of a thrift store bin for a buck or two. She loved finding old, thrashed and forgotten horror books. It was her favorite reading material by far. Her exposed skin now covered in goosebumps from the breeze of daybreak, every second of which she loved. Myrna welcomed the chill. The breeze was revitalizing.

After a deep shower that seemed to take forever, Mitch finally emerged from the stucco restroom building. His wet hair combed neatly over the back of his head, a fresh pair of jeans, black tee and neatly fitting jacket covering his clean body. In his hands, a plastic grocery store bag held the bloody garments from the night before to be discarded. Just behind the picnic table was a stone trash receptacle, topped with a lid made of metal. Mitch shoved the bag through the opening, pushing it deep into the bin with the rest of the refuse. From his back pocket he pulled out a book of matches. He struck one, followed by another, and another, dropping each flickering flame into the trash bin. Soon, smoke would billow from each opening of the metal top, as the contents inside burned to nothing more than ash.

"Come on," He said with a nod of the head. "Let's get rolling."

"You're gonna leave that thing burning out here all by itself?"

"Look around you. It's nothing but sand and dirt as far as the eye can see. What's going to burn? Besides, we'll be miles away. Not our problem. Let's go."

Myrna kept her nose buried deep inside her paperback as they continued the hours-long drive to Eureka, California. She felt it inappropriate to push on and on about the details of the night before, regardless of how curious she might be. No matter how badly she wanted to scratch that itch inside her brain, she felt best to let it go. As weird as it truly might be, it was her brother's job, after all. He probably didn't want to talk about it. She figured it would be like someone pestering their parents about how their day was at the office. To an outsider, it might seem exciting. To the person living it in real time, borefest. Besides, the more details he spilled, the more comfortable he became divulging information about his activities, which could in time come back to bite him. She didn't want that, of course. It was her brother, and killer or not, she loved his stupid ass. Though she didn't want to be that typical, annoying little sister, she wanted to connect with him. That wouldn't happen if she remained silent with her face buried in a book for the duration of this drive.

"So, you know this book I'm reading?"

"You mean the one in your hands *literally* right now?"

"Yeah, this one."

"Right. Yeah, I can see it."

"It's kinda funny. The bad guy in this book, right? He's a dude who lives out in the desert and he just sort of sits out there, waiting for people to come to him."

"Yeah, so?"

"Well, let me finish. So, he waits for people to come to him and when they do, he murders them, cooks their flesh and serves it to people unsuspectingly."

"Jesus, Myrna," Mitch said, disgusted. "What the hell is wrong with you? You read that shit?"

"Yeah, it's great! It made me think, you and him would probably be buddies. You know, if he was real and all that."

"No, no. I don't think so."

"Well, why not?"

"I don't cook and eat people! Who do you think I am?"

"Oh no, not that," She said, waving him away. "I just meant, you know, the killing and stuff. You two could, like, *talk shop*. Maybe exchange war stories."

"Sure, Myrna. Sure, why not. If he ever shows up, tell him I'll buy him a cup of coffee and pick his brain."

Myrna settled into her seat, slinking down a bit more than normal. She looked at her feet, keeping her head down, allowing her jet black hair to cover her face. A sense of nervousness had overtaken her as she took a series of deep breaths.

"Hey Mitch?" She asked, keeping her eyes off of him. When she finally got the nerve, she looked at him. "Can I talk to you about something?"

"Sure, what do you want to talk about now? Cannibals underwater? Or, no! Cannibals in space, maybe?"

"No, shut up. I'm serious. There's something I've been wanting to tell you. It's been, I don't know, bugging me, I guess you could say."

"Alright. What is it?"

Myrna puffed her chest, her lungs filling with oxygen as she gathered the courage to speak. Her shoulders lifting and falling with each inhale and exhale, again, her eyes breaking contact with him.

"You remember that trouble I got in a while back? What we talked about at the burger stand? The robbery and all that?"

"Of course."

"I wasn't completely honest with you about that whole thing. And I'm really sorry, but I lied to you."

"What do you mean? What was the lie, exactly?"

"Well," She filled her lungs again with oxygen courage. "The truth is, Deidre and I *did* bust into that rich girl's party. And it's true, we snuck into her parent's bedroom. There was a safe, it was behind this huge painting on the wall, and the safe was unlocked. I swear it was! Mitch, you have to believe me, we didn't break into the safe, OK? Well, when we opened it we found all kinds of crazy shit inside. Jewelry, a gun, wads of cash. And I mean *lots* of cash. And the necklace was in there."

"Wait, what are you trying to tell me, Myrna? You did in fact rip that family off? You stole that necklace?"

She remained silent for a moment, every fiber of her being rattling like a rattlesnake's tail when a hiker kicks a rock into its path. She hung her head lower than she ever had. At that moment, she felt so ashamed. So ashamed of not only stealing a priceless necklace from a family that did nothing to her, but also for lying to the one person who'd always had her back.

"Yes," She whispered in shame. "I did. I stole it, OK? Look, I'm not proud of myself for it. But yes, I took it."

"Why Myrna? Why would you steal from them? What have they ever done to you?"

"I don't know, shit, Mitch. I was angry. I've always *been* angry. Ever since you grew up and moved away, I've just felt so fucking alone. Do you know how that feels? To feel completely alone in a world that seems to want *nothing* to do with you? Every fucking day I feel this sense of such nothingness. Like I just don't matter."

"Of course you matter! I couldn't stay living at Grandma's forever, you know? And one day you will move out, too."

"I know, I get that. But that's all I have. Grandma. And, I know deep down she loves me and all that. But she never signed up for this. To raise you and I both. And you at least had 14 or so good years with our parents. I can't even remember them, for fuck's sake. All I have is pictures. No actual, tangible memories. Just fading photographs and Grandma's fading memory to tell me stories."

They remained silent for a few moments, the only sound in the car, the hum of the electrical engine a few feet in front of them. Mitch said nothing, he just nodded his head as he processed the information being dropped onto his lap. Not knowing what to say, he remained quiet, letting her pour her feelings out like a dam that a bomb had hit.

"Do you know what it's like to be me, Mitch? People hate me just because I *am* me. The weird girl who likes scary movies and music that isn't made on a computer in some basement somewhere. I don't know, dude. Maybe I was just looking for attention. Maybe I'm just a lifelong fuck up. A problem child. Some orphan left to be forgotten by time."

"Why are you telling me all of this now?" He finally asked.

"Well," She paused for a moment. "You opened up to me about being a killer. About your tendencies, and how you turned it into, basically a job. A *weird* fucking job, but a job all the same."

They shared a laugh together, which felt good to both of them.

"I felt, if you could share something like that with me. Then I should be able to share anything with you, too. And that's probably my biggest secret. So, there you have it. I did it, OK? I stole the fucking necklace."

"Where is the necklace now?"

"It's in a safe place. Somewhere no one will ever find it unless I want them to."

"You can't tell me that much?"

"One secret for one secret, that's how it works, right?" She asked with a sly smile. "Another time maybe. For now, that secret is safe with me."

"You know that necklace you stole is priceless, right? It's worth millions. You understand that?"

"Yup. That's why it's in a safe spot only I can access."

They each broke into a smile, both feeling somehow relieved at this outpouring of honesty and truth. As though a firewall had broken down between them, where they felt they could tell each other anything and everything. Right then, they'd never felt closer to one another, and it felt good. Right then, they felt like a true family.

"Well, I'm glad you told me. Thank you for being so honest. It really means a lot," He said, patting her leg. "You know, believe it or not, I was bullied a lot as a kid."

"Really? I didn't know that."

"Well, we're in a safe space. We're sharing things, right? There was this group of dudes in high school. They used to pick on me all the time. They called me Mitch the Bitch."

"Oh my god," Myrna laughed, covering her mouth. "I'll have to remember that one."

"Don't you dare call me that!" He said, pointing a stern finger at her. He quickly broke into a laugh. "They once duct taped me to the handball courts with my pants down. The entire girls PE class came out and saw. It was terrible."

Myrna's head cocked back from a deep belly laugh, clapping her hands together in pure joy.

"Oh my god, that's too much. I'm sorry, I don't mean to laugh."

"No, it's OK. Looking back, it is kind of funny, right?"

"Yeah, it is," She said, snorting as she laughed. "What did you end up doing about it?"

"I put a knife through one of their necks and cut his entire throat out," He said matter-of-factly, clicking the blinker to change lanes on the freeway as Myrna's laughs turned quickly to gasps.

CHAPTER 26

Three hours southeast of their destination of Eureka, California, Mitch pulled into a gargantuan truck stop off the 299 Freeway close to Iron Mountain Road. The Excalibur Travel Center stretched close to a full city block, its parking lot of scorching hot, black pavement as far as the eye could see. The monstrous building was built to resemble an old castle, the perfectly imperfect brick facade climbing high towards the clouds amongst the scattered pine trees that surrounded it. At the far end of the property, stalls taller than big rigs stood, allowing for long-road truckers to park, sleep, refuel as well as wash themselves and their prize possession trucks. The fake castle itself was home to a multitude of different fast-food joints creating an impressive food court which wrapped around the biggest mini-mart that Mitch or Myrna had ever experienced. The parking lot was packed with different vehicles fighting their way to settle in next to gas pumps. Mitch, not needing to refuel thanks to his expensive Zeus electric vehicle, could bypass the mayhem, driving past the mass crowds towards the back of the lot. There, they found the scarce, yet wide-open and available charging stations. As Mitch settled the car next to the robotic looking device, he shut down the engine, stretching his lower back in the seat.

"How long will this take?" Myrna asked, not looking at her brother, flipping through her smartphone.

"Not long," He said, his voice breaking into a yawn. "These things have a quick charge feature. Shouldn't be but an hour or so, tops. Why? You've got somewhere to be?"

"Yeah, I do," She said, lowering her sunglasses, glaring at him through the top of her eyes. "Eureka, remember?"

"Oh, I remember. You just seem quite eager all of a sudden. That's all."

"The closer I get, the more anxious I become."

It was true. The closer the destination came, the more her blood boiled with anticipation. She couldn't believe that what she'd dreamt of for so long could become true. A reality she'd never expected to face. A *man* she'd never expected to face. But now, being so close, it's like she could smell the evil wafting through the air towards her. Like a cartoon fox, a strong aroma filled with a lifetime of hate floating down the freeway from Eureka, landing a direct hit into her nostrils, leading the path to her eventual prey. With each sniff, she felt more and more intoxicated by the scent. He was getting closer, and she could feel it in her spirit as it burned more and more with each mile they traveled.

"Calm your nerves, kid," He said, propping open the driver door. "We'll be on our way in no time. It's a good opportunity to grab some food, stock up on some caffeine. Hit the bathroom. All the road trip essentials."

Mitch inserted a credit card into the futuristic-looking device, paying the fee and connecting the charging wand into the front of the car. A subtle ding noise shot from the device, as the connection sent a fresh charge to the batteries within.

"I thought you said we should be inconspicuous?" Myrna blurted out, nodding at the credit card as Mitch slid it back into his wallet.

"Oh, this?" He asked, showing the front of the card to his inquisitive sister. "It's a fake. Doesn't have my name on it. But I'm proud of you for mentioning it. Now you're thinking like a killer."

They joined in with the hordes of zombie looking travelers headed inside the castle. When electronic sensors picked up their movement, two sliding glass doors shot open allowing them entry. A blower from overhead burst to life covering their bodies with recycled, stale air. The smell inside was anything but comforting or inviting. The stench of travelers on the road for way too long floated all around, intermingled with the heavy odor of chemical cleaners all too familiar in these roadside establishments. Like some sort of bionic lemons grown in a laboratory somewhere that had fallen into a batch of acid and ammonia.

"What sounds good?" Mitch asked her, rubbing his hands together, surveying the food court options.

"*None* of this, to be honest," She said, a look of mild disgust on her face.

"Well, it's this or nothing, Myrna. Take your pick."

"So, you're saying nothing *is* an option?"

"Eat something, wise ass. I'm buying. Just decide."

Myrna had already expected him to buy lunch. In fact, she'd fully expected him to pay for everything on this trip. Not only was she still a teenager, but, they both knew full well he'd just cashed in on a briefcase of 40 grand cash. If he couldn't pony up for a sandwich or a burrito, that would be a real problem.

Amongst the fried chicken fingers, the poor excuse for Mexican food and the greasy hamburgers was a shining gem stone. What would normally never grab the attention of a hungry human in the wild stood out amongst these atrocities like a beacon of hope. A treasure chest of sliced meats, fresh vegetables and baked bread. A sandwich joint named The Port.

"Fine, how about The Port?" She offered. "At least we won't end up sick from a turkey sandwich, right?"

"I hope not," Mitch said through a deep breath. "The Port it is."

After placing their order at the counter, the two sat across from one another waiting for their sandwiches to arrive. It didn't matter to Myrna how long they took. Suffering the boring, hour long wait now, followed by devouring a turkey sub would make the time seem to go quicker, she'd hoped. Rather spend the final moments in that truck stop doing something, like devouring a turkey club, rather than staring at the wall or constantly checking social media, only to see the same six posts repeatedly. Hopefully chewing away at lunch would help make the time seem to pass quicker.

"So, do you feel ready?" Mitch asked, breaking the silence between them.

"For what? A turkey club? Sure, why not. It's a sandwich."

"No, stupid," He said, shaking his head. "For Eureka. For *him*."

"I thought we weren't supposed to talk about this in the open," She whispered.

"Look around you," He said, surveying the inside of the food court. "Who's listening to us now?"

She tapped her fingers on the formica table, her eyes floating around the room, nervous. She bit her bottom lip.

"I don't know," She said under her breath. She looked at her brother. "Is anyone ever really ready for this? I mean, I know I *want* to do it. I *have* to do it. But am I ready?" She shrugged.

"You'll be fine," He said, reaching across the table, clasping her hands in his. "Besides, you've got the best teacher in the game. And I'll be there with you, guiding the way the entire time."

She nodded, her eyes unable to look at her brother. As she looked around the food court, way off to the other side of the room sitting next to the window was a boy. He looked about Myrna's age, and his eyes were locked dead onto her. The strange boy was cute, she thought. He had a similar vibe to Myrna, that sort of modern punk rock and roll aesthetic. His hair combed in a sort of pompadour, a worn out denim vest covered the band t-shirt he wore. The vest was plastered with all kinds of band patches, different buttons and plenty of snags and tears. He sipped from a soda cup and when he noticed Myrna looking his way, he sent a million-dollar smile in her direction. Myrna, confused about what to do, sent an awkward smile back. She felt a bit of a flutter within her chest, happy to have a momentary connection with someone outside of her brother for a moment. A connection that had nothing to do with death. When she lost track of how long she'd been staring, a red, plastic tray hit the table and it brought her back to her own reality.

"One turkey club on white and one Italian with no mayo," The Port employee said. "You need anything else?"

"No, this will do. Thank you," Mitch said.

Myrna reached for her sandwich, unwrapping it slowly from the white paper. Quickly she glanced back to the boy, his eyes still locked in on her. When she looked again, he smiled at her once more. This time, she smiled back with confidence.

"Hey," Mitch said, trying to grab her attention. "Hey!"

Myrna finally looked towards her brother, her mouth wide open knowing she'd been caught flirting from afar. She lifted her sandwich, taking a massive bite. Mitch watched her for a moment, then looked across the room at the boy. Mitch purposefully stared him down, but the boy didn't care. His eyes remained locked on Myrna, unfazed. He continued to look, smiling the entire time, dodging Mitch's imaginary daggers now flying across the food court.

"How's the sandwich?" Mitch groaned, taking a bite of his own.

"It's good," She said, her mouth full. "Very, uh, *good*. How's yours?"

"It's fine," Mitch said. "Just, hurry and eat. We need to get back on the road."

When Mitch looked the other way, Myrna's eyes again wandered to the far side of the room. She batted her eyes at the boy, sending another playful smile. Then, she turned to Mitch, who was still staring in the opposite direction into the mini-mart. She figured he hadn't seen, and besides, she really didn't care. What's the harm in a little playful flirting, she thought?

CHAPTER 27

They finished their sandwiches in record time, which, unfortunately meant they now had to begin the painful wait for the car to finish charging. Mitch played with his phone, frantically clicking away at the touch screen. He was right in the middle of some sort of business, Myrna assumed, and she had no intention of interrupting. Mitch had been acting weird, anyway. On this leg of the drive, ever since they left Reno, he'd acted differently. She couldn't quite put her finger on it, but he seemed off. Not himself anymore. Aside from their short connection about the stolen necklace, he had been short with her, quick to react, and seemed sort of touchy. Though, she figured, in his line of work, always looking over your shoulder for either a cop or someone hired to take you out, she felt his feelings were justified. So, she let it go. Thought nothing of it. She definitely didn't want to interrupt whatever he was clearly in the middle of now as he continued to flip through tabs on his smartphone.

Myrna again looked to the other side of the food court at the mystery boy. While they finished their sandwiches, he hadn't moved from the booth. There he sat, flipping away at his own smartphone glancing towards Myrna when it seemed convenient to do so. As she stared at him from afar, he slowly turned his head towards her. *Damn, he caught me,* she thought, twisting her head away. A playful smile washed over her face, as her black hair fell forward, protecting her blushing from the world. She looked back through the stringy, black curtain of hair to see him laughing in her direction.

Pushing her hair behind her left ear, their eyes met, and they stayed locked into one another's gaze. This time, she felt even less concerned if Mitch caught her. It was all in good fun. Harmless. He could deal with it. Just then, like an electric charge had been sent through their table's bench, Mitch jumped, dropping his phone onto the table. He ran his hands over the top of his head, letting out a deep, frustrated sigh.

"You all through here or what?"

He grabbed the plastic tray, yanking it from the table.

"Yeah, damn," She replied, recoiling. "What's your deal, dude?"

"Nothing, nothing," He said, rubbing his eyes. "I just want to get the fuck out of here already. I'm feeling way too cooped up."

His eyes scanned the room, looking through the opened doors to the mini-mart.

"Do you need anything for the drive? I'm gonna walk around a bit. Stock up on some shit so when the time comes, we can just *go.*"

"Sure, thanks," She said, confusion rattling in her tone. "Just a bottle of water, the good stuff, please. Nothing with the logo of this place on it. And maybe some, I dunno. Some of those rainbow sour rope thingies. Oh, and a pack of gum."

"Alright," He sighed, standing from the booth.

Mitch moved towards the doorway, dumping the trash from their lunch into a waste bin, placing the plastic tray on top. He moved into the mini-mart, hit yet again by the enticing smells of chemicals pretending to be cleaner. On the left was a long, black counter. Three spots were open for cashiers to ring up snacks, sodas and castle themed souvenirs. The center of the mart had rows and rows of different snack foods; beef jerky, nuts, different flavored chips and any kind of candy you could imagine. Towards the back, more rows of shelves composed of road essentials. Some jumper cables, bottles of motor oils, car accessories and paper goods. Wrapping the back wall was an array of glass doors displaying cold drinks from sodas, to teas, to the water bottles Myrna had requested. The right side of the mart provided a coffee center with different baked goods promising they were made fresh in house.

Mitch loitered the aisles, picking out a plastic bag of rainbow colored sour ropes for his sister. He pretended to be looking for something else, some unknown item, as he watched Myrna from afar. Soon, just as he expected, he watched as the mystery boy rose from his booth, sauntering over like Joe Cool to his lonely, innocent sister. He watched as the boy approached her, motioning for an invitation to take a seat. His blood boiled hotter and hotter as he watched Myrna give the OK, the boy taking a seat across from her.

Mitch moved to the cooler doors, picking out a bottle of trendy water. All the while, glancing over his shoulder way too obviously at the two of them. He watched as they spoke to one another, leading into laughs and playful chatter. From another cooler door, Mitch grabbed two bottles of ice cold cola, then, walking into another aisle picked out some beef jerky. Two flavors, teriyaki and original. He made his way to the counter, keeping his eye on this mysterious teen who was attempting to woo his little sister.

"That'll be 26.35, sir," The clerk said.

"Huh, What?" Mitch couldn't focus, his attention stuck on the two teenagers in the food court.

"26.35," The clerk repeated in an unfriendly tone.

"Oh, wait," Mitch said, shaking his head. "This too. A pack of gum."

"28.19," The clerk told him the new price.

Mitch dropped thirty dollars cash onto the counter as the clerk bagged the items. He tore the bag from the clerk's hands, dashing back to the table where they sat. When he arrived, both Myrna and the boy were mid-laughter together. Clearly, they were getting along well, making Mitch seethe.

"Hey Myrna," Mitch said, towering over the table like a storm cloud. "I got the stuff."

"Oh, Mitch!" She shouted through laughter. "This, this is my brother Mitch. Meet Sam."

"Hey Mitch, good to meet you," Sam said, reaching out his right hand.

Mitch glared at him, refusing to shake the boy's hand.

"Good to meet you," He said, anger throttling his voice. "Myrna, I'm gonna go put this stuff in the car and check the charge. You going to be ready to go soon?"

"Oh yeah, of course. Let me use the bathroom then I'll be ready to go."

He followed his sister out of the food court into the mini-mart walking behind her at a frantic pace.

"Stay away from that boy," He muttered, his teeth clenched tight.

"Why?" Myrna laughed. "He's harmless. I'm just having a little fun with him."

"Look," He said, turning so they were face to face. "Use the bathroom and tell this dude to take a fucking hike. We need to get rolling."

"Alright, Mr. Protective. Geez."

"I'll be back in a minute. Meet me right here."

Mitch stormed through the sliding, mechanical glass doors as Myrna made her way towards the back of the building. In the far back, down a long white hallway plastered with employee notices and posters were the restrooms. If it were at all possible, the stench of chemicals and cleaner was even stronger within that hallway. So strong, it almost choked the breath out of you.

Mitch stomped his way to the car, leering at every traveler as though they were an enemy on his list. It was as though he was challenging anyone who wanted or was willing to try him. A walking threat to anyone who dared look at him sideways. When he reached the car, he noticed it hadn't fully charged. His impatience was working against him.

"Dammit," He grunted.

He threw open the passenger door, dropping the bag of items onto the seat. Slamming the door, he hightailed it towards the front of the truck stop. When he entered, he saw Myrna leaning against the counter next to the coffee machines, her cell phone held in both of her hands. Sam stood awfully close to her holding his phone as well. He kept his distance for a moment, when he saw Sam put his cell in the back pocket of his jeans. Sam then made his way towards the back of the building towards the restrooms. Mitch was pleased to see him retreat. He bounced over to Myrna, a dopey smile covering her young face.

"I'm gonna hit the restroom and we can be on our way. Cool?"

"Sure thing," She said, boasting a happy grin, staring at her phone.

Mitch marched down the hallway with purpose in his eyes, maneuvering out of the way as a portly man exited the bathroom, pushing his way past Mitch. He glanced down the hall to ensure no one else was coming his way, then propped the restroom door ajar with his foot. When he glanced inside, he saw Sam standing at a urinal relieving himself. The bathroom was quiet, empty, aside from the sound of Sam doing his duty. Mitch rushed inside and without wasting a single second, he grabbed the boy by his collar.

"Hey, what the fuck, man!" Sam shouted, pulled from the urinal.

"Shut the fuck up," Mitch said, his teeth clenched so tightly, he could've broken them out at the root.

Mitch tossed the boy into the biggest of the three stalls, slamming the door shut, locking it behind him. From under the wall of the stall, the boy's feet danced across the ground as Mitch's remained calmly still, planted firmly into the filthy tile floor. They wrestled for a moment, when the groans of the boy changed to something resembling a wet gurgle. The sound of a blade pulverizing flesh echoed throughout the room, as the slash sounds bounced off the tiled walls. Over and over, the sound of a knife stabbing through flesh as Sam's breath grew faint. His cries fell to whimpers as he fought through the blood flowing within his throat for the ability to breathe. One last stab came from above, as Mitch forced the blade to crack through Sam's skull, stabbing his brain. Just then, the boy's body went completely limp. Mitch positioned his flopping, lifeless body to sit upright on the toilet, so anyone coming in would see his boots and imagine it was someone handling their business. Mitch then fell to the floor, crawling out of the stall across the floor. He stood, tore off his blood splattered jacket, wrapping it into a ball inside out. He rushed to the sink, scrubbing the blood from his hands, dousing them in soap and rubbing them frantically underneath the piping hot water. Grabbing a paper towel, he held it under the running water, wiping his neck and face to remove any splatter that may have splashed him. He tore off more paper towels, rubbed his hands dry, using them to open the bathroom door. As he approached Myrna, he held his jacket inside out, drying his wet hands as though it was any normal bathroom visit.

"You ready?" He asked, tossing the towel into a trash can.

"Sure," Myrna said. She looked around her brother. "Where's Sam? I wanted to say goodbye."

"He's gonna be in there awhile, if you catch my drift." Mitch waved his hand under his nose.

"Oh god. *Gross*," Myrna said, a look of disgust on his face. "Alright, fuck him. Let's roll."

A few moments later, a man dressed in tight blue jeans, a white tank top and a cowboy hat entered the restroom of the Excalibur. As he unzipped his jeans at the urinal, he stared up at the ceiling. When he had his business finished, he looked towards the ground as he zipped back up. Flooding the tile from underneath the largest stall was a massive pool of blood. It had flowed and accumulated around his boots, coating them in dark, warm crimson. The man jumped back, screaming at the top of his lungs. A clerk burst through the door, seeing the pool of blood that had covered the tile floor, flowing like water from a broken pipe. He kicked the stall door open, and there, sitting on the toilet, stab wounds covering his chest and a fatal wound at his forehead were the blood-soaked remains of Sam. A permanent state of fear locked on his young face, his limbs dangling from his torso like a forgotten rag doll in someone's attic.

As police and paramedics stormed the Excalibur, Mitch and Myrna were already long gone. Traveling at normal speed, headed towards Eureka. Within hours, they'd arrive, bringing even more death along with them.

CHAPTER 28

The sun still hung high in the daytime sky as they rolled into the city of Eureka. A quaint, seaside town in Northern California, Eureka is well known for its gorgeous, historic, Victorian homes and its proximity to Sequoia Park. The park is the home of many massive and splendid redwood trees. Myrna sat low in her chair, her dark sunglasses hiding her eyes from the world. Her expression didn't change even slightly as they drove through Eureka towards the understated downtown area. A scowl remained on her face, her black hair framing it perfectly, with strands falling over her sunglasses. Mitch didn't say a word as he drove, either. In fact, he had said little if anything on the final leg of the drive. Aside from a few frantic text messages, which he responded to the instant they arrived on his phone, he kept to himself. The only proof of life coming from Mitch was every once in a while, he'd shift his position. Myrna figured his ass and legs were tired from the tedious and non-stop drive of the road trip. She didn't blame him; hers were too. She wanted out of that car. Though being held hostage in a seedy motel yet again wasn't much of an escape from the luxurious seats and fresh smelling air conditioning of Mitch's Zeus X-1. As Mitch turned left into the Castaway Inn, Myrna's eyes darted all around to take in her surroundings. She couldn't believe it. A beautiful, boutique Victorian style hotel. Not a motel, mind you. A *hotel*. A real, classic hotel. She rubbed her eyes to ensure she saw an H on the sign. No, it couldn't be. Mitch must have something planned here. Something to do with the job at hand that awaited them.

Maybe he needed to use the business center for something relating to the endless text messages that kept his phone chiming the last 30 miles.

"Why," She stuttered a bit in shock. "Why are we pulling in here?"

"We're staying here tonight," Mitch said, his tone showing zero emotion.

Myrna couldn't believe what she was hearing. If she weren't so surprised, his lack of emotion might have appeared offensive. Her scowl quickly transformed on its own to a half smile. As the car crept through the parking lot, she gazed in wonderment through the windshield at the gorgeous building. Freshly painted white walls trimmed with gorgeous, sunny yellows. Three floors, each window graced with beautiful, white blinds draped elegantly. Not shutters or rags coated in years of cigarette smoke. These were real drapes. Like the ones in pricey magazines detailing houses owned by the rich and famous you'd see in the checkout line at the grocery store. The amazing architecture sang a song from centuries past. Tonight, she imagined, she'd sleep like the well-to-do sleep. When she laid her head this evening, she'd do so as a goth princess, like she always knew she truly was.

"Are you serious? But, why? I thought you said we needed to keep a low profile? Motels? Not *hotels*."

"I changed my mind, alright?" He barked. "Besides. We both need a good night's rest. This place should give us that. And, what the hell? You deserve a bit of niceness once in a while."

"Gee, thanks, brother."

As he put the car into park, turning off the engine, he let out a small laugh. The first sign of emotion he'd shown for hours. Myrna, overjoyed by the show of kindness, laughed right along with him, her face now in a bright, amazing smile.

"Come on. Let's check in," Mitch said, nodding his head towards the entrance.

When they entered the Castaway they weren't met with musty old carpet, foul lobby restrooms that were overused and under cleaned or any other dank and disgusting stenches they'd become accustomed to. No, the lobby of the Castaway smelled fresh, like a perfect spring day on the beach. Fresh-cut flowers sat in two separate vases decorating either side of the marble check-in counter. The yellow and white tiled floor had been freshly mopped, and the carpet leading towards a dining area beyond the check-in counter was as clean as the day it was originally installed. An older woman wearing a black blazer with gold buttons over a pressed white shirt approached the counter.

"Good afternoon! And welcome to the Castaway," She boasted. A friendly smile that could've warmed even the coldest of hearts on her face.

"We'd like to check in, please," Mitch said, his tired face returning the best smile he could muster.

"I can help with that," She said, clicking away at a keyboard. "Reservation? Or looking for a room?"

"Looking," Mitch said, leaning into the counter. "Say, do you have one of those suites available?"

"A suite?" Myrna asked, her face impressed.

"You're in luck," The woman said with a smile.

She took the Graves kids through the proper rigamarole of checking into a hotel, giving them the standard spiel about check-out times, breakfast being served, when the pool closed. After papers were signed and cash had been exchanged, the woman handed two card keys across the counter inside a white, glossy envelope.

"Enjoy your stay. My name is Mona. If you need anything, call me right here at the desk."

"Thanks, Mona. We should be fine," Mitch said, taking the keys.

The suite at the Castaway was on the third floor at the end of the hallway far from the noise of the elevator or any other guests. The entryway was secured by two heavy, wooden, carved doors painted stark white.

"Like to do the honors?" Mitch asked, handing Myrna a key card.

She ripped it from his hands in a flash, licking her lips as though she was a predator whose prey hid behind those wooden doors. When she pushed them open, she was in awe. White carpet laced with golden accents stretched the entire room. To the immediate left, a master bathroom unlike anything she'd ever seen. Inside, marble floors met with marble counters with an elegant jacuzzi tub next to an all glass shower. Past the bathroom, a king sized bed decked in soft, white linens. Against the right wall a glass door opened into a second room where another king sized bed pushed against the wall. Double glass doors opened to a small balcony overlooking downtown, allowing the soft, delicious breeze from the ocean to enter and cleanse the room.

"Holy shit, Mitch," Myrna said, dropping herself onto the closest bed. "This room is incredible. I can't believe you did this."

"Why not, right? We're not gonna live forever. Might as well enjoy it while we can."

Mitch walked through the suite, entering the second bedroom and dropping his duffel bag and the leather case containing his recent cash score onto the bed. He tore off his shoes as he wrestled himself onto the bed. When Myrna entered, his head was on the pillow, both of his arms underneath his neck, his eyes closed.

"Hey Mitch," Myrna said, her fingertips just barely tickling the door frame. "I just wanted to say thank you. You know, for this. And, *not only* for this. For everything. I wasn't sure at first, but, the closer we got to Eureka, and the more we opened up to each other. The more right this feels, you know?"

He shuffled, moving his head, lifting it slightly to make eye contact with his sister. He smiled at her.

"It's going to be great, kid. Trust me. Once this is all said and done. You're going to feel like an entirely new person."

"I know, I know," She said, looking at her feet.

"Hey, don't be scared. I'm going to be there with you through it all. I won't let that monster do anything to you. Trust me."

Myrna smiled at him, resting her body into the door.

"Now, we both need some rest. You mind if I take a nap?"

"No, no. Not at all. I might put that tub to use, to be honest. That thing looks inviting as fuck."

Mitch chuckled. They did not build this elegant space for the likes of Myrna Graves.

"Good for you, kid. Enjoy yourself."

***

After a long, warm bath, Myrna threw on the softest robe she'd ever felt in her short life. It was like wearing a cloud pulled from the heavens. Warm, cushy, cozy. She would steal that when they left, that much she was sure of. It was her brother's name on the room, not hers. He had the money to cover it. So fuck it, she thought. She rested on her bed, sinking deep into the pillowy mattress as she drifted off to a relaxing sleep. She had left the doors to the patio wide open, allowing the street noise and the cool, subtle breeze from the ocean to drift her into dreamland.

She wasn't sure how long she slept, though it had to have been at least a few hours, as when she awoke, the sun had disappeared, the moon now hanging high over the West Coast. She woke thanks to the light in the main room erupting to life. As she blinked feverishly, rubbing and hoping her eyes would adjust to this new normal, a slight hint of annoyance crept in. When the blur dissipated, she saw her brother pacing the room next to her bed. The more he moved back and forth over the same spot, she worried he'd blaze a trail that would remain forever.

"Come on, wake up," He said in a normal tone.

"What the fuck, dude? I was in such a deep sleep."

"Too bad," He said, twirling his knife in his right hand. "You've always got to be alert. I could've killed you right where you were laying."

"So?" She asked, sitting up, still in the cloud soft robe. "When you slept earlier, I could've killed *you*, too. What of it?"

"Touche," He said, pointing the tip of his knife in her direction. "Now come on, get up. Get dressed. It's time for another lesson."

"What lesson?"

"I'm going to test you. I want *you* to show *me* what I taught you a few days ago."

Myrna stomped into the bathroom like a scorned child, changing clothes as quickly as she could. She emerged wearing a white Black Flag t-shirt and a pair of red athletic shorts with white trim down the sides. Her black hair flowing over her shoulders and in every which way, completely unkempt.

"You ready?"

"For what?" She asked, her arms out in confusion. "I still don't know what we're doing."

"Grab your knife, already. *Damn.* I have to explain *everything*?"

From within her backpack, Myrna retrieved her knife. She tore it from the sheath, holding it so the blade pointed down awkwardly.

"Ok, now what?"

Mitch approached, standing directly in front of her. So close, she could feel the warmth of his breath over her face.

"With a knife, you can only be as far away as your arms allow. Got it? So, you're going to be close to this piece of shit."

"Got it," She said, a coy smile on her face.

"This isn't funny. It's serious. Now, if you want to strike me with a fatal hit, where do you stab?"

"The balls!" She leaned over with laughter.

"Come on, this shit isn't a joke, Myrna. When you're face to face with this guy, it's life and death. Yours or his."

"OK, OK," She said. She sucked in a deep breath, lifting her shoulders. When she exhaled, her shoulders dropped as she turned her head, stretching her neck muscles. "I can hit you in the *heart*," She positioned the tip of her knife over Mitch's heart. "That will kill you. Fatal hit. I can stab you in the *brain*," She held the knife to the side of his head, the point pressing ever so slightly into the flesh underneath his hair. "That's what we call zombie style."

"*We call*? OK, got it." He laughed.

"I can," She dropped to one knee, pressing the blade into his upper thigh. "Cut *here*, straight through the artery. That's the messy one, you'll bleed out. *A lot*. Also very fatal."

"Good," Mitch said, nodding.

"Or, I can," She turned her brother's body, placing the knife against his throat from behind. "Slice your throat. The *deeper* the *better*. Cut all the way until I feel fucking bone. Take your damn head *clean* off," She whispered into his ear.

"Good for you," He said, turning around to face her. "You remembered. That's excellent. Now, will you remember it when it counts?"

"Never count out a strong woman who's fucking pissed off, Brother," She said, admiring her blade, twirling it slowly in front of her eyes. She looked back at him. "It could be the biggest mistake of your life."

He nodded as a smile appeared on his face. At that moment, she felt pride oozing from her brother's spirit. It made her happy. Truly, she was elated. They had officially bonded in a deeper, more meaningful way anyone would ever believe. Death can do that to you.

"That concludes your lesson for the night," Mitch said, sheathing his weapon. "Now, let's go get dinner. All this talk of killing has got my motor running, and I'm hungry."

CHAPTER 29

A few blocks down the road from the Castaway sat the Bayside Cafe. A small, 24-hour diner that served breakfast all day and had a menu that stretched miles. Mitch didn't care where they ate, really, nor did Myrna. As long as the food was decent and the coffee was hot, it would do just fine. Lining the beach side diner on one side was vinyl booths colored sky blue and white. The opposite side, a dining counter, something neither of them had seen in as long as they could remember. With short, steel stools bolted into the linoleum flooring, the tops covered in chipped vinyl that matched the booths. From behind the counter, staff poured hot coffee into mugs for old timers. Gray-haired men and women who probably had no place else to go. Choosing to not interrupt those at the counter, the Graves kids nestled comfortably into one of the many empty booths.

"What'll it *be*? What'll it be?" Mitch asked, skimming the abundant menu. "Breakfast any time? I'm sold. I love breakfast at any time."

"I wish more places did that," Myrna agreed. "Like brother, like sister, huh?"

They shared a laugh at their similar love for breakfast foods.

When the waitress arrived to take their order, Mitch quickly shouted out his—eggs benedict, hash browns and wheat toast. As Mitch said, no one makes a benedict like a sketchy looking diner in a small town. Myrna went with the corned beef hash, eggs over easy, hash browns and white bread toast. And when Mitch told the waitress to keep the hot coffee flowing all night long, Myrna agreed. There they sat, sipping diner coffee by the pot, chatting about their lives. The past, where they'd been, where they'd hope to go in the future. Everything but the task that awaited them the following night. After nothing but lessons and chatter of death and murder, Myrna was happy with the conversation. For the first time in a while, it was nice to feel as though she had more of a brother in Mitch and less of a homicidal teacher. After Mitch's silent treatment on the drive, his openness and ability to communicate with his sister was refreshing. She welcomed it. It was something that she deeply appreciated.

"So," Myrna said, taking a fork full of corned beef and eggs. She spoke with her mouth rudely full. "What can you tell me about our parents? You had so much time with them. And I, well, I don't remember them at all."

"They were cool," Mitch said, opening a creamer packet and pouring it into his coffee. "Dad was a pharmacist, which you knew. He owned his own store. Mom was a stay at home mom, and really, she took care of everything. For all of us."

"Were they kind?"

"Oh yeah. Mom was sweet as pie. She was full of love. And, I can tell you with absolute certainty you were everything to her, Myrna. You were the apple of her eye. She was so happy when you came home from the hospital. I don't think she even looked at me for weeks."

"Oh, shut up. That's not true."

"I'm serious," He said, biting his eggs. "She loved you. Dad, too."

"God, I wish I would've had some time with them. To get to know them even the tiniest bit. I'm so," She grunted, clenching her fists. "Fucking *angry* that monster took them away from us."

"I know. It's terrible. There isn't a day that passes that I don't think of them. I wish they were here, now. Well, not in this diner. But you get what I mean."

The table went quiet for a moment, for the first time since they had sat down together. Mitch continued to eat, as Myrna sort of toyed with her food. The look on her face grew more and more intense as the seconds ticked by.

"Say, Myrna," Mitch said, washing down another bite of food with steaming coffee. "I asked once, but I have to ask again. Call it curiosity, I don't know. Call it whatever you'd like. But, I've got to know. Where are you hiding that necklace?"

Myrna froze, glaring across the table at him. She held her fork upright, no longer playing with the food, just allowing it to grow cold.

"I told you. It's in a safe place. Don't worry about it."

"Why can't you tell me?" Mitch asked, his pitch higher than before. "It's *me*, Myrna. Your brother. I thought we could tell each other anything."

"We can," She said, spinning her fork again in the sticky egg yolk. "But, I don't know. I'd rather keep this one to myself. I feel safer that way."

"You know, it might make you feel better to get it off your chest. To tell someone. It might help you sleep at night."

"I sleep *fine* at night, thank you."

"Consider me a therapist. Sometimes, just getting shit off your chest is a good thing. It stops it from weighing you down."

"It's not weighing me down at all. Actually, I'm quite at peace with the entire situation. Why do you keep bringing this up, anyway? What? You want to take it and sell it? Another *score* for you?"

"Whoa, Myrna," He said, dropping his fork, putting his hands up in defense mode. "Not at all. Stop it. Like I said, I'm just endlessly curious. That's all. I mean, what does a 16-year-old girl do with a priceless diamond necklace?"

"Well, stop being so curious and let it go. I don't want to talk about it."

"OK, fine," He slammed his forearms onto the table, shaking his head. "I'm just saying, if you told someone. Told *me*. I think it could *really* help you in the long run."

"Forget about it, Mitch," She said as sternly as she could. "Let's just finish our food and get back to the hotel."

Silently, they finished their respective meals, and at the end, Mitch paid in cash leaving a generous tip before they pushed through the glass doors into the cold, ocean air. They didn't say another word to one another as they walked back to the Castaway. Myrna kept her distance, her arms crossed at her chest. When they entered the room, Myrna immediately pushed into the bathroom slamming the door behind her. With her palms planted into the marble counter, she stared at herself in the mirror. The girl looking back at her was now someone she almost didn't recognize anymore. It was as though she was staring at someone new. A scarier, angrier version of herself. She wiped a tear from her left eye before throwing on the hotel robe. It was the only thing at that moment that seemed to wash away the discomfort that had taken such an intense hold on her.

She pushed open the bathroom door and jumped under the covers without saying a word as Mitch entered the bathroom to go about his nightly routine. There she laid, listening to the running water of the old pipes within those Victorian walls, and the creaks and cracks put her mind at ease. She had drifted close to sleep when Mitch emerged, shutting off the light in the room.

"Goodnight, Myrna. Sleep well," He said. "Tomorrow's a big day for the both of us."

"I know," She said through sniffles, wiping her nose with the back of her hand.

"And Myrna," He whispered, pulling the door to his room closed. "I'm sorry if I upset you. Sleep tight, kid."

CHAPTER 30

Myrna slept, though it was anything but a normal, peaceful sleep. Even though she was in fact asleep, her mind never truly rested as it ran through one horrific scenario after the next, flashing her with visions of monsters, blood, death and destruction. Her mind's eye took her dream state hostage while the horrific events of what happened to her parents all those years ago played out in real time right before her eyes. Having no recollection of the events, not even knowing her parents aside from the stories old photographs and her grandma had told, her imagination had to fill in those blanks. And, when your mind is at play, anything can happen. Left to your own imagination, nightmares play not only within your head, they become all too real. Almost like you can reach out and touch them, slicing your fingertips on the memories.

While she tossed and turned, inside her head she saw visions of a faceless man larger than life towering over her loving mother and father in their old home. His hands must've been like a catcher's mitt, large enough to crack a skull like a grapefruit within its fingers. Muscles bulging from underneath tattered, filthy rags, a monster so strong that no man or woman could ever counter his blows. His callous, vicious attacks. From outside of her own body, she could see herself standing in their master bedroom doorway, watching as this monster had his way with her beloved parents. Forced to watch as the people who gave her life, had their lives stripped and torn from their bodies. Their souls torn apart piece by piece before her very eyes.

The giant, faceless man held a knife into the air. Its blade must've been over a foot long. She watched as the monster held her father by his throat, choking the light from his eyes. He dug the shimmering blade into her father's chest, directly through his heart.

"*FATAL*," She whispered in her sleep, tossing to one side of the bed.

As he removed the blade from his body, it dripped crimson across the floor, spurting and dousing the monster's torso in warm, copper smelling liquid. She watched as the monster thrust the blade into Mr. Graves' throat. He pushed with enormous pressure, digging deep into the flesh of his neck, sliding it to one side as flesh and tendon flew across the room splattering the far wall.

"*FATAL*," She whispered again, thrashing underneath the covers.

When the man turned to her cowering mother, Myrna's fists clenched tightly, both in her dream state and as she laid in bed. Her hands crumpled the covers deep within her fingers, so tight, she could have torn the blankets to shreds. She could see the light beaming from within her mother's eyes along with pure, absolute horror. The man shoved the blade into her mother's gut once, twice. Again and again, he dug it into her flesh, blood and bile coating his massive hands as it dripped and sprayed all around them.

"*IT'LL TAKE TOO LONG*," She whispered, thrashing again. "*NO, NOT FATAL. SHE'S SUFFERING!*"

The man twisted his head on his shoulders as though it had dislodged from his neck, turning around completely to look at Myrna. She could feel the flames burning within those eyes as they burned holes through her body. It felt like her skin had become engulfed in flames as he gazed upon her. The man smiled. A disgusting, crooked smile of shattered, blackened teeth. Myrna knew the man could see her in the room, watching as he continued to pulverize Mrs. Graves torso with slash after slash.

"Myrna!" She heard her mother scream. "Save Myrna! Save the baby! Don't hurt my baby!"

She looked to her mother, watching the agony grow on her face. Then, her mother opened her eyes to look directly at her daughter. Their eyes remained locked, as Myrna watched the light within those eyes go black and all warmth in her spirit grew ice cold, transforming into two sockets dark as the darkest of any night.

"NO! NO! LET HER GO!" Myrna screamed, thrashing back and forth under the covers. Trying with all of her might, every muscle in her body to break through this nightmare and save them. Save her parents and kill that son of a bitch right there in that room once and for all. When she woke, Mitch was sitting on the bed next to her. His hands gripped her shoulders as he shook her.

"Myrna! Myrna wake up!" He screamed. So close, spittle splashed her face from his lips.

When she woke, she woke up screaming and shrieking. Clawing at her brother, wanting nothing more than to tear the soul from another living being and cut it to ribbons.

"WHERE IS HE? WHERE IS HE?" She screamed, her eyes darting around the room.

"You were having a nightmare, kid. That's all that was. It's OK. I've got you. I'm here."

She crashed into her brother's arms, tears pouring down her face. She cried and she cried, unlike any cry she'd ever done. Mitch could feel her body quaking in his arms. He tried to hold her, to comfort her, but nothing he did would stop her body from shaking. She planted her palms into his chest, pushing herself away. She looked into his eyes, tears flooding her cheeks.

"We've got to kill that motherfucker, Mitch," She said, sniffling. "I'm ready. I'm *so* fucking ready. I want to tear him limb from *fucking* limb if it's the last thing I do."

CHAPTER 31

Loud banging and commotion from the adjacent room woke Mitch from his own deep sleep. Throwing off the covers, he sat on the edge of the bed, rubbed his eyes and let out a deep, tiresome yawn. Gently, he opened the door to Myrna's room. When he entered, she stood in front of the tall dresser staring at the wall as a coffee pot spurted hot, metallic liquid.

"Morning," Mitch said, nervous in his tone. "You doing OK?"

"You want coffee?" She asked blankly, not taking her eyes off the painted wall.

"Please," He said, another yawn. "So, do you want to talk about what happened last night?"

"No." She said, flatter than her previous words.

"Come on," He said, sitting in an armchair in the corner. "That was pretty intense. You don't want to talk through it?"

"No, I do not."

"You know, it seems there's a lot you want to keep from me as of late," He said, smug as shit, crossing his arms.

"Yeah, and?"

"Well, I thought we shared shit. No secrets."

"Since *when*?"

"I guess I just assumed it, OK?" His patience was wearing thin.

"You don't have any secrets? Huh, Mitch? Anything you want to tell *me*?"

He remained quiet, his eyes drifting to his feet.

"I thought so," She snipped.

She filled two coffee mugs with steaming hot beverage, handing one to him without making eye contact. Sitting upon her bed she crossed her legs, clicking on the television, taking long sips of the coffee.

"So, what? We're just not gonna talk?"

"We can talk. I'm not *mad* at you. I just don't want to talk about *that*."

The TV roared on, Myrna clicking through the guide looking for something specific. When she found the right channel, she leaned her body against the headboard letting out a deep, relaxing sigh, taking another sip of coffee.

"What is this? *Forensic Files*? Turn that off."

"No. I love this show."

"I don't enjoy watching shit like this. Come on," He stood, reaching for the remote.

"Tsk, Tsk, Tsk," She mouthed, looking him up and down. Her eyes sent a silent threat to her brother. "Why don't you like it? It shows how one day you're gonna get caught?"

"Yeah, don't joke about that Myrna."

He returned to the armchair, sitting deep within the cushion, holding the mug with both hands close to his face. Leaning his head against the back of the chair he closed his eyes. Myrna finished her coffee, jumping from the covers to refill her cup before climbing back into bed.

"So, what's the plan for today? How do we approach this?"

"Tsk, Tsk, Tsk," He mouthed at her, a smartass grin on his face. "The plan will come together in due time. It'll all go down tonight. Things are in motion."

"Can you tell me the plan? You want me to go in blind?"

"You won't go in blind. We'll discuss it, every single tedious fucking step of it. This is my job. I take it very seriously. I never leave anything up to chance."

"Well, I'm ready."

"I'm well aware," He said. He lifted his head from the back of the chair. "Today, we're going to relax. Relax as much as we can. But first, we need to make a stop in town."

"Yeah, what for this time?" She sipped her coffee, her eyes fixated on the true crime tv show.

"Need to get you an outfit. Something good for killing," He said, rising from the chair. He sipped the coffee before he spoke. "If you're gonna play the part, you need to dress the part. We can't have you waltzing in with those punk t-shirts and cut-off jeans, now can we?"

CHAPTER 32

Mitch found an Army Supply store just outside of Eureka in the neighboring town of Rosewood. The supply run was a short drive through city streets giving them plenty of time after this quick chore to relax at the hotel, regain their strength and settle their nerves before nightfall. Holding the steel framed glass door, Mitch allowed Myrna to enter the storefront. The shop owners had filled the clothing racks inside with camo gear, old metal items of war and various weaponry. Once inside, Mitch nodded his head towards the back of the shop, urging Myrna to follow his lead. At the far back was a rack of full body jumpsuits. Mitch flipped through the choices, finally pulling a black suit into view.

"Here we go, this should do it," He said, holding it against Myrna's body.

"What the hell is this? Some sort of James Bond mission or something?"

"You can never be too careful, kid. Try it on."

Myrna slipped behind a sketchy looking curtain into the tiniest changing room she'd ever seen. She tucked her legs into the jumpsuit, pulling it over her torso, stretching her arms in. Reaching back she zipped it up along her spine. The room, equipped with a slim mirror, allowed her to check out the suit. It covered her entire body from collarbone to her ankles. Along the front straps allowed the one wearing it to hold on to different items of attack. Smaller openings, she assumed, were for extra bullets. The larger slots, she didn't even want to think about what might fit in those. She wasn't trying to be Rambo. This all felt like overkill to her. But, her brother was the professional, her mentor. He knew the ropes far better than she could ever pretend. When she tore the curtain away, she stepped out into the musky stench of the surplus store.

"Oh hell yeah," Mitch shouted. "Now that's bad ass. You see yourself? You look like a fucking mercenary."

"Is that what we're going for or something?"

"Yeah, kind of," He said, stepping behind her. "How's the fit? Too tight? Too loose?"

"No, it's weirdly comfortable, to be honest. I could probably sleep in this thing. It's like a onesie."

Mitch laughed and shook his head at the comparison.

"OK, now, try this on with it."

Mitch handed her a ski mask fixed with holes for the eyes and the mouth.

"No fucking way!" Myrna blurted, stepping away from him. "What is this? Some sort of stupid caper costume? This isn't a fucking movie, Mitch."

"No shit, stupid," He said, his hands on his hips. "Just put it on, for fucks sake."

Reluctantly, she took the mask, pulling it over her head. There she stood, draped in black, looking as though she was about ready to rob a bank.

"This is so stupid, dude," She said, staring at herself in the mirror.

"No, it's perfect. *You're* stupid. OK, take it off. Let's buy this shit and get outta here."

She tore the mask from her head, pushing it hard into his stomach. She fixed her hair that was now a mess, making her way to the changing room. Before she entered, she turned back to him.

"Wait, you're not getting any of this stuff?"

"Don't need it," He said calmly. "I've got stuff. I'm the pro, remember?"

She twisted her head, rolled her eyes and entered the changing room.

***

The rest of the day both Mitch and Myrna remained quiet as death itself. Mitch remained in his respective room resting, listening to music on a pair of headphones and, every so often, pacing the room and punching the air as he moved. It was clear he was preparing himself for what was to come. Trying, almost too hard, it seemed, to pump himself up. Myrna wasn't nearly as calm. She laid in bed; the covers pulled to her chin like a child hiding from the boogeyman deep in thought. Thinking about everything and nothing all at once. About her parents, running a slideshow in her mind of every fading photograph they had ever shown her that she could remember. Thinking about the man, whoever he may be. Thinking about her nightmare, wondering if this man could really be as large as her mind led her to believe and when the time came, did she really have what it would take to pull this off. Was she ready for this? To become a murderer. The weight of that thought pulled her down like an anchor. But, most of all, she thought about how she would finally kill the son of a bitch and how great it might feel to know the deed had been done.

To Myrna's chagrin, the day sped by. Faster than any day Myrna could remember. It was as though life was on fast forward. Like fate and destiny had sped up time to get her closer to the end goal. While she appreciated the sentiment, her nerves were now firing on all cylinders, and, as much as she wanted to do this, she felt like she needed more time. More than ever before, she questioned if she was in fact ready for this. But it was now, or it was never. And with her brother now walking through that bedroom door, his leather suitcase and duffle bag in hand, she knew the time was now. She'd have to be ready. It was life and death. And this motherfucker had already buried two Graves' family members. She'd be damned if he did it to a third or a fourth.

"It's go time," Mitch said, his voice low, solemn. "You ready?"

"I think so," She whispered.

"Get dressed," He instructed, nodding his head at the jumpsuit still waiting for her in the plastic bag. "It's time to go over the plan."

As Myrna slipped into the jumpsuit, Mitch sat in the armchair spelling out everything step by step. He tells her that when they arrive, they'll park the car far down the road making the rest of the trek on foot. *"Can't leave the car too close,"* He told her. *"Too many eyes could see it out front. Too risky."*

He pulled out a printed map, an overhead view of the house. Mitch tells her she will move to the back of the house, where his intel had led him to believe the back door will be unlocked. *"This guys a killer. And a stupid, clumsy one at that. I hear he never locks his doors. It's like he invites intruders. He welcomes them."* He explains. There, she will wait for his signal. Upon getting his signal, she was told to burst into the house like a bat out of hell, run through the kitchen into the connecting living room where Mitch will wait for her with the man. With *him*. Mitch will take on immobilizing him and ensuring that Myrna won't get hurt. From there, Mitch will guide her through the entire process, slice by fucking slice.

"But, how are you going to get inside?" She asked, her face as serious as a heart attack.

"Don't concern yourself with anything but the plan of your own. Follow what I'm telling you to do and follow it *exactly* as I'm telling you. If you worry about me, if you wonder what if, if you think of anything but what I've told you, this can not work. You got it?"

"I got it."

As they left the Castaway Hotel, Mitch clicked open the trunk, dropping both his duffel bag and the leather case inside. Myrna, following suit, dumped her backpack next to them. Mitch unzipped his bag, pulling his silver revolver from inside. He tucked it into the back of his pants as he slammed the trunk shut.

"You've got your knife ready?"

"Check," She said.

"OK," He said, letting out a deep sigh. "It's time to rock and roll, kid."

They entered the vehicle, Mitch firing the engine over, pulling out in a skid. This was it. Now, there was no turning back.

CHAPTER 33

Mitch pulled the car next to the curb, shut down the headlights and turned off the engine. It finally made sense to Myrna why he had such a silly vehicle. The damn thing ran silent. He could sneak up on and get away from anyone without issue. To her, he was a true pro. He must've really thought of everything. She felt then like everything he'd said was all true. Mitch had really meant every word of what he'd told her, and that made her finally feel at ease. Her nerves settled and though she was so close to confronting the man who'd killed her parents, she felt awkwardly calm. Way more calm than she'd expected. This happening to her, it felt like a far-off, distant dream. All her life she'd wanted to get her hands on this monster. To exact revenge, *true* revenge, on the man who killed their parents. The man who stole her life from her. He was so close, the scent of evil struck her and she knew that his time had come. His life had run its course, and she would ensure that any light within his eyes would be snuffed out before sunrise.

"Come on," Mitch whispered, crouching down slightly beside the car. "Follow me. Stay as close to the trees as you can. Fewer eyes to see us."

He waved his right hand through the air, pointing down towards a curve in the road. Small, single story ranch-style homes lined one side of the street. Across the street, just up from the curb, a wall of dirt shot upwards. At the top, a thick line of trees and shrubs cast heavy shadows over that side of the street. Perfect cover for two intruders dressed entirely in black. Though Mitch didn't have the jumpsuit, he wore black athletic pants and a black, pullover hoodie. Myrna didn't think to question him. He was the pro after all, and she trusted him with her own life.

About one block around the curve in the road, Mitch knelt close to the curb staying hidden deep within the shadows. Pressing his hand outward, he stopped Myrna to pull her in close so they could speak quietly to one another. She knelt as he whispered into her ear.

"That's the house. That one, right there," He pointed.

Across the street was a yellow stucco house with a brown-tiled roof. The tiles were ragged and falling off, and the house appeared to be in a sad state of disrepair. The yard was all dirt and weeds and the driveway asphalt seemed beyond repair, cracked in too many areas to count. Resting in the driveway was a beat-up car which appeared to be well past its expiration date. Just past the yard was a small staircase with an iron rail leading to the front door. The front door faced the driveway, and the huge window covered in some sort of cloth blocking any view in or out of the home faced towards the main street. Above the staircase, a flickering, dying bulb cast a sad, dim light over the front of the home.

Myrna's body quaked. She couldn't believe she stood right across the street from the man who'd killed her parents. Nothing more than a hop, skip and a jump away from *him*. Just a mere few yards stood between them meeting face to face, and if she had her way, it would be the last time they ever did so. Mitch could feel the buzz emanating from her body as he rested his hand on her shoulder.

"Look, I know you're excited. But keep to the plan. Do not stray. Trust me. Shit could go south real fucking quick if you go off script."

"Don't worry," She assured him. "I'm locked in. I'm ready."

"OK, throw your mask on and head around the right side of the house. There's a chain-link fence there, but it's decrepit. You'll be able to weasel through it with ease. Go to the back door and wait for my signal. Through the window of the back door, you'll be able to see the lights from the front room. When the lights go out, you run in like a bat out of hell straight to that room to meet me. I'll be there waiting for you."

"Got it," She said. "Hey, I love you, Brother. Stay safe, OK?"

"I love you too, kid," He said with a smile. "You do the same."

Myrna slipped the intruder mask over her head, taking off towards the side of the house. She kept herself low to the ground and remained well within the shadows of the trees. Once she passed the house, she took off towards the front lawn. Keeping her knees low, she crept across the dirt lot, stopping when she could reach out and touch the stucco wall. Just to the side of the house, as her brother told her, was a decrepit, chain fence. Carefully, she pushed the chain link away, first, slipping her left leg through to the other side. Next, she knelt low, bringing her torso and head through, followed by her right leg. Right above her was a small window that looked into the kitchen of the home. With her back to the wall, she crept quiet as a field mouse, until she reached a set of 3 stairs that led to the back door. The wooden door, just like Mitch said, had a pane of glass at the top. With her finger tips tickling the door, carefully, she peered in through the glass.

Across the house sitting in a rotting old recliner, it was him. The man who'd taken everything from her family. The son of a bitch who'd slaughtered her parents without care. Her blood boiled as she watched him. There he was, rocking back and forth, a can of beer in his right hand. The top of his head was almost completely bald, the hair that remained composed of a sad comb over and some straggly strands that fell down towards the back of his collar. His face, cracked and old, covered in unkempt, gray stubble. A pair of light wash jeans and a white tank top covered his thick body. He wasn't even remotely close to as big as her nightmares had led her to believe, nevertheless he was decent in size. Large enough to be a problem for someone of her stature. At this moment, or when shit hit the fan, size meant nothing. No man of any size could stifle the rage that now boiled underneath her skin. If she could get her hands on him, she felt as though she could rip his head clean off with only her bare hands.

As she remained at the door, she saw the man stand from the recliner making his way towards a hallway that led to the back of the house. She recoiled, dropping underneath the pane of glass, when her shoulder nudged the handle. The door lurched open, as she stared directly into the kitchen of the home.

"Fuck, fuck," She whispered to herself panicked. "This wasn't part of the plan, Mitch. Now what?"

Her eyes darted side to side, as the warmth of the home enveloped her body. She could feel the evil emanating from inside, washing over her like she'd been poisoned.

"Fuck the plan," She muttered.

Jumping to her feet, she charged inside. When her feet hit the linoleum floor of the kitchen, as quietly and carefully as she could, she pushed the back door so it appeared closed. The man was still nowhere to be seen, as he had retreated to somewhere deep inside the home. The kitchen counter stretched from the back door around the left of the room, finishing with a small inlet on the opposite side of the kitchen. Underneath the counter was a dishwasher unit. Remaining low to the ground, she darted towards the counter, nestling close to the appliance. Her heart beat so fast inside her chest, it surprised her he didn't hear it from across the house. Surprised he didn't think someone was knocking at the front door. And just then, at the front door, came a series of loud, deep thuds. To her utter dismay, someone had actually begun knocking on the front door.

"Oh shit, oh shit," She whispered, her eyes darting all over the kitchen. She pressed her body against the cabinets as footsteps approached from down the hall.

"Hold on, god dammit," The man's voice rang out, filled with gravel, like the man had been choked close to death by the grip of nicotine and tar. "I'm coming, I'm coming."

Myrna closed her eyes, pressing the balls of her feet deep into the fake tiled flooring. She pushed her back hard into the dishwashing appliance, her arms outstretched on either side of her body as though she was trying to grasp something while holding on for dear life. Just as she heard the front door open, she looked at the back door. The way from where she'd come. *Should I run for it? This isn't part of the fucking plan! We're caught! We're dead, oh my god we're so dead. He's going to kill us too. Both of us. He's going to wipe out our entire family. This can't be happening!* The front door opened, creaking and cracking as it did.

"What the *fuck,* man?" He yelled. "Where the fuck've you been? You're two days late, you know that! What the fuck is the boss gonna say when he finds out the job ain't done, huh?"

She heard a new pair of footsteps enter the house. Someone was inside with the man. Myrna's heart raced. She gripped the handle of her knife, dragging it from the sheath. Holding it close to her chest, she took in a series of loud breaths, trying to calm herself. Trying to find the right answer and what to do next. When the man spoke again, Myrna couldn't believe what she heard.

"You know, Mitch. If the boss is pissed about this, I'm blaming you, pal. I'm not taking the fall for this shit."

"Mitch?" Myrna whispered to herself. "What the fuck is happening?"

"Don't you worry about the boss," Mitch said, shutting the door behind him as he entered. "I've got the boss under control. You just leave all of that to me."

CHAPTER 34

Myrna crawled as close to the edge of the cabinets as she could without coming into view. Her ears had perked up, trying to listen to every word, every single syllable that came from that room. She was absolutely confused beyond words. Why was Mitch acting so familiar with him? How was he able to just waltz in the front door like he was visiting an old friend? How did he know Mitch's fucking *name?* None of this made an ounce of sense, but she couldn't stray from her position. The only thing she was certain of was that Mitch had her back. He wouldn't let any harm befall Myrna. She trusted him, and he loved her. She knew it.

"We were supposed to handle that Reno job two days ago, Mitch," The man said, frantically moving about the living room. "There was a timeline attached to that job, or don't you fucking remember that?"

"No, no, I remember," Mitch said. "The timeline's changed. The Boss cleared it himself. We're in the clear."

"Yeah, well, we'd better be," The gravel filled voice choked out, accompanied by a series of deep coughs. "Probably for the better anyway."

"Why's that?"

"I lost my damn pistol," The man groaned.

"Your pistol?" Mitch asked. "What pistol?"

"My pistol. You know the one, *my* pistol. The silver revolver? You've seen it a million times, dickweed. It's got my name stamped in the barrel in pure gold."

"Name stamped on the side in gold," Myrna whispered to herself. "Stamped in *gold?*"

"Well, I'm sure it'll turn up at some point. Don't stress about it too much. It's just a gun," Mitch said, dismissing him completely.

"Yeah, yeah. Easy for you to say. You run around with these, fucking, thingamajigs that the kid's like to use these days. Powerful pistols all for show. Mine is a *real* pistol. A man's *pistol.*"

Myrna gasped, her eyes shooting wide open. It was then that she remembered Mitch sitting at the table in that sleazy motel room, polishing a silver revolver with gold letters stamped into the side. She remembered it like it happened ten minutes ago. The image tattooed inside her memory. She never could figure out why Mitch had a gun with those letters stamped into the barrel. Even Mitch himself refused to divulge that information.

"Al," She whispered to herself.

That was *his* gun. *His* pistol. The pistol belonged to *him*. And his name was Al. She tore the mask from her head, dropping it to her feet. She couldn't fix her jaw into place if her life depended on it. What the fuck was happening? It felt like the world was caving in from all sides.

"Either way, I got a friend on the force. He runs the downtown division. He hooked me up with some unregistered pistol he nabbed off a gang member or some shit. Definitely a good connection to keep. I'll introduce you to him."

"Sounds great," Mitch said, clapping his hands together. "So, Al. I was thinking–"

Mitch's sentence never ended. It just trailed off into the ether, syllables floating through the air without a home. That's when he saw her.

"Oh shit," Mitch groaned.

Al, bent over next to his recliner, turned and looked towards the kitchen. Standing in the doorway was Myrna, unmasked, a scowl stained on her face. Her knife, held in her right hand, dangled toward the floor.

"Who the *fuck* are you, bitch?" Al shouted, standing upright. He lifted a black pistol from his right pointing it towards her. He screamed, "What the fuck are you doing in my house!"

"Myrna, *NO!*"

Al pulled back on the trigger as Myrna ducked, covering her head with her arms. Mitch, lunging forward, pulled Al's pistol from the back of his pants, striking him across the back of the head. When the shot rang out, Al recoiled from the blow, the bullet striking the door frame just to Myrna's right, missing her entirely. The blow was so severe, Al dropped to his knees and covered the back of his head with his now shaking hands. In his right, he still held the black pistol.

"Mitch, what the *fuck* are you doing, man?"

"Put the fucking gun down, Al. Do it, *right now!*"

Mitch moved around his cowering body, Al's signature pistol now pointed at his head. Al lifted his right arm, dropping the pistol onto the stained carpet, his left hand firmly pressed into the back of his head as blood trickled through his fingers, spilling down the back of his neck.

"Mitch, what the *fuck* is going on, man?"

"Shut up, Al," Mitch said calmly. "We've got some business to attend to here. But don't worry, you're the man of the hour."

Mitch lifted his right hand high above his body, thrusting downward, striking Al again and again in the top of the head with the handle of his own pistol. Al fell to his stomach whimpering in pain. Blood pooled around him as it dripped over his face and through his fingers. He rolled to his back, staring up at Mitch, a crooked smile appearing on his face.

"You piece of pond scum," Al said, spitting up at Mitch. "You come into my house and beat me with my own gun. You're a dead man. They're gonna kill you for this."

"I don't think so, Al," Mitch said, looking towards Myrna.

She remained crouched in the doorframe, terrified beyond thought. Watching in terror as her brother transformed into an entirely new person before her eyes. A violent, horrifying person. As she watched, her hands covered her wide open mouth as he beat the brakes off the man who she wanted nothing more than to see dead.

"Come on, Myrna," He said, wiping his mouth with the back of his hand, blood smearing across his face. "Come on, get it over with. We need to get outta here already. Neighbors definitely heard that gunshot. *Come on, kid!*"

Slowly, she lifted herself to her feet, moving in short steps towards them in the living room. Mitch held the pistol trained on Al as Myrna inched closer and closer.

"It's OK, Myrna. You're safe. I promise. Now, just like I taught you, OK? I'm here with you. I'll guide you through the entire thing."

"What the fuck are you talking about, Mitch?"

"Shut the fuck up, Al!" Mitch shouted, kicking him in the ribs. "Myrna, do it. This is what you've always wanted. Here he is. This is *him*. We *found* him. Now, *kill* him!"

"Kill me?" Al laughed through coughs, rolling a bit on his back. "You know you can't kill me. The boss will have your ass, and it'll be you that will wind up dead."

"What is he talking about, Mitch?" Myrna asked, standing nervously, keeping a safe distance.

"Come on, Myrna. Forget him. He's insane. Just do what I told you. Just like we practiced."

"Don't listen to him, girly," Al said. "You lay a finger on me, and you'll both be dead by morning."

Mitch transferred the pistol from his left hand to his right, keeping it trained on Al. He moved close to Myrna, grabbing the back of her head, pushing his face right against hers.

"Now is your chance, kid," He whispered. "This is what you've always wanted. What you've always dreamt of. Getting your revenge. Killing the man who killed our parents. You can't back out now. We've come too far. It's now or never. Life and death, remember? You don't take his, he will take both of ours. Come on, you've got this. Remember your nightmare? You want him to bury two more from the Graves family? Wipe us off the planet?"

Myrna looked at Al. This frail, gross old man. Blood pouring from the back of his head, his body trembling while trying to keep his composure. Trying through it all to remain the tough guy. Then, she did as her brother told. She couldn't stop thinking of the night before. Her nightmare. The visions that played in her mind of the knife stabbing her father in the heart. The never ending slashes against her mother's stomach, bile and guts spilling to the carpet of their bedroom. This is the man who did that. The monster knelt before her. *This is him*. Her face changed from fear to fury. Grasping the handle of the knife, she knelt down, straddling the man's chest.

"Get the fuck off me, girly! I swear, don't listen to this man. *He's nuts!* He's gonna get you both killed!"

"Shut the fuck up!" Myrna screamed with all her might. She lifted the knife into the air, her hands wrapped around the handle, swinging it down and sinking it into his stomach.

Al gasped in pain. His mouth jutting open, his hands reaching for the knife, trying to remove it from his flesh. Myrna held it inside of him, pushing and pushing it deeper and deeper inside, tickling his guts with the sharp blade. After twisting it a few times, she tore it from his gut, blood and bile streaming into the air behind it.

"Mitch," Al begged. His voice, frail and losing strength. "Shoot her. Get her off of me, Mitch. Please."

"No can do, pal," Mitch said, the pistol still trained on his head.

Myrna looked at the man, grabbed him by the jaw, forcing him to look back at her. To look her dead in the eyes. She wanted to see every ounce of evil inside this man as she tore his soul apart.

"I've been waiting all my life for this moment," she whispered, shaking her head as her eyes welled with tears. "I'm so tired from imagining all the ways I would kill you. How I would end your pitiful life. You killed my parents, you motherfucker. *Our* parents! And today, we finally give you what you've deserved for so long."

"*Our* parents?" Al whispered, his voice getting weaker by the second. "Wait. No, it can't be."

Mitch's eyes stayed locked on Al, as Al studied his face from below.

"It is," Al whispered, a smile growing through the pain on his face. "I can't believe I didn't recognize you before. It's you. It *is* you. You're the kid. The kid from the train tracks. All this time, you've been right under my nose and I never put it together." He coughed, a small spattering of blood bursting from his lips.

Myrna's head slowly turned towards Mitch. Her eyes, filled with confusion, hate, anger. She glared at him, as he refused to make eye contact with his sister.

"What is he talking about, Mitch?"

"No more secrets, right, Myrna?" Mitch asked, taking a deep breath. "You remember how I told you someone taught me how to kill? Taught me how to indulge my deepest desires? Well, this is him. This is the man who taught me everything I know. The same man who murdered our parents 16 years ago."

CHAPTER 35

Myrna was stunned. A revelation she never saw coming from the man she trusted most in this world. The one she trusted most with her life. Now, telling her that after all this time, he'd known the man who killed their parents personally. As Al bled out, Myrna remained straddling his chest, holding the knife, ready to strike. But at that moment, she didn't know which of them to strike next.

"You knew, all this time?" Myrna asked.

"No. *No,* Myrna," He said, his face looking sincere. "I only found him about a year or two ago. I almost killed him myself, a couple of times actually. But come on, admit it. This is so much better! You and I? Brother and sister? Finally, taking out the fucking garbage that killed our parents?"

Myrna's hate shifted back to Al. Writhing in pain, Al stared into Myrna's furious eyes. His hands pressed into his gut, ichor and warmth flooded from the open wound thanks to Myrna's blade.

"Whatever you do," Al choked out, blood appearing against his filthy teeth. "It ain't gonna bring them back, honey."

"You're right," Myrna said, her eyes dropping. Her hair falling over his face like a shield. She popped her head back, a level of anger in her eyes that most humans have never witnessed. "But I *can* put your sorry ass into the fucking grave!"

She lifted the knife high above her head, swinging it down, stabbing the blade straight through his chest, diving directly into his cold, black heart.

She twisted the blade from side to side, her teeth clenched tight, shrieking in his face, nose to nose, keeping her eyes locked onto his.

"I want to watch the light fade from your eyes!" She screamed. "Just like you did to my mother, my father! I want to witness your soul leave your disgusting body! *Die you motherfucker!*"

After pulling the knife from his chest, she lifted it again, and with one loud scream and one deep slash, she sliced clear through his neck. Cutting all the way to the bone. She stood above Al, next to Mitch, watching as Al squirmed like a fish left on the deck of a boat on a warm, summer day. His body flopped for a moment, until his eyes rolled to the back of his head as he laid, soaking in a pool of his own, warm blood. She kept her murderous glare locked on his eyes as they faded, rolling to pure white. That was something she wanted to remember. A memory that would spring into her brain every night she laid down to sleep. A memory, while utterly terrifying to most, would lull her to sleep with a smile washed over her face for the rest of her life.

"There," She said, taking deep breaths. "It's done."

"How do you feel?" Mitch asked, looking at his sister proudly.

Myrna remained silent for a moment, admiring the work she'd done at her feet. She nodded to herself, clearly proud of a job well done.

"I feel," She paused. *"Alive."*

"That's my girl," Mitch said, patting her on the back. "Good work, kid. You did real good. And, look at you. You got out pretty much unscathed, too? Not bad. You might just be a natural like me."

"Well, I had a good teacher," She smiled at him.

Mitch wrapped his arm around her, pulling her in tight, as she rested her head against his chest.

"I'm proud of you, kid," He said. "Oh, and by the way. Happy birthday."

They both shared a laugh, looking over the dead body of the man who had taken their parent's from them all those years ago. It had all finally come to an end. 16 years of nightmares and demons haunting her, following every step she took. Now, the monster is gone. Myrna had slayed the dragon. She patted her brother on the back as she moved across the living room towards the kitchen.

"So, what do we do now?" She asked, her back to her brother. She sheathed her blade, strapping it back to her hip. "Do we just leave the body here? Or do we need to dispose of it? Because honestly, I don't know if I'm ready for the advanced course of cutting up a body. Oh, and you know we're going to need a long, and I mean *long* conversation about all the shit you never told me about this guy. You're lucky I don't stab you next for keeping that information from me."

From behind her, across the room, Myrna heard a loud clicking sound. Her ears perked up, feeling frozen where she stood. Slowly, she turned around to face Mitch. There he remained, standing next to Al's dead body, the hammer pulled back on the silver revolver, pointed directly at his sister's head.

"Not so fast," Mitch said. "Tsk Tsk Tsk, my sweet little sister. Unfortunately, we have a little more business to attend to here. Drop the knife, nice and slow. And keep your fucking hands where I can see them."

CHAPTER 36

Myrna couldn't move. Not only for fear of being shot, of course, that now seemed like a real possibility. But she froze in pure fear with her arms raised, wrists at her ears, her jaw falling towards the floor. She was shocked, stunned, terrified beyond belief. Her mind raced a million miles a minute, as that revolver remained trained right between her eyes from across the room.

"Mitch, what the fuck–"

"Shut it, Myrna," Mitch shouted, waving the gun in the air, directing her to move towards him. "Not too fast. Slowly. Don't even think about making a move, or I'll blow your head off where you stand."

"Mitch, are you fucking joking? It's, it's me. Myrna. Your sister."

"Yes, Myrna, I'm well aware of who you are. Now please, if you don't mind. Move your skinny ass over here the way I told you. I want to get this over with and get as far away from here as I can."

Myrna, her hands in the air, moved across the room to her brother. He motioned with the gun for her to kneel in front of him. She did. Her eyes never left his, as she sat on the back of her feet, her hands behind her head.

"No secrets, right? No secrets between brother and sister? Isn't that what you said? OK. That's fine. I'll tell you everything. Here's the truth, Myrna," Mitch said, turning, stepping away from her. He turned back, the gun held steadily towards her face. "It's true, Al killed our parents. You got him. He's dead, and *you* killed him. Just like I promised. It's also true that, yes, he is the one who taught me to kill when I was a kid. Back on the train tracks. I met him again a little over a year ago when they chose me to handle a hit for my boss. It was a two-man job, and Al was the other gunner teamed up with me. I didn't have a choice, and I couldn't back out or they'd have killed me. Oh, I knew it was him right away. The shitty hair, that voice. I mean, those evil eyes have been burned into my fucking skull since I was 14 years old."

Myrna's eyes welled as her bottom lip quivered and a set of tears fell down her cheeks. She watched as Mitch paced the room in front of her spilling his guts. Sharing his darkest secrets with her.

"We work for the same boss. And when I say boss, I'm sure you understand, *mafia*. The mob. We're both hired killers for the same mob family. When I was a kid, I thought he was just some scumbag drifter who killed drug addicts and lowlifes just to get off. To come up on some drugs or money or something. But I was wrong. Oh boy, was I wrong. I found out later, Al is an ex-cop. He found it much more lucrative to be on *this* side of the law, rather than enforcing it. He had me lure people from the neighborhood so he could kill them, and then he'd rob them blind later that same night. I had no idea but once I met him, I got to know him. It all made perfect sense."

"Did you," Myrna cut in, her voice cracking through the tears. "Did you lure mom and dad to him?"

"Not intentionally," Mitch said, shaking his head. "I'm not proud of this shit, Myrna. I have to live with the fact that I got our parents killed. You think *you* have nightmares?" He laughed. "They've been haunting my dreams since the night he killed them."

Mitch walked closer, kicking Al's dead body repeatedly. On the final kick, they both heard a snap come from Al, Mitch clearly breaking a couple of his ribs in the outburst.

"That night, he told me to meet him at the train tracks. He had a job for me. But I now know it was his perfect way to get me out of the house so he could do what he does. When I came home, I found him in the bedroom. Dad was already dead, and I tried to save mom. But I was fucking 14. He nearly killed me in the process. I'd made the mistake of telling him Dad owned his own pharmacy. That's the whole reason he took me in. It's why he latched on to me and why he allowed me to get so close to him. It was all a ruse, Myrna. A perfectly calculated ruse to rob mom and dad."

He knelt down in front of his sister pushing his face so close their noses touched. She could feel the breath as it wafted over his lips.

"After he killed them, he stole Dad's car, drove to the pharmacy and robbed us blind. He had the keys, so he walked right on in. Cool as a cucumber, walked out with 15 grand of dad's money, *our* money, in his pocket. And all the pills and drugs he could ever dream of. The alarms didn't even go off. All in a day's work, huh?"

He stood again, walked to the opposite side of the room, continuing to pace.

"So then, this Reno job comes up. Another two-man job, no big deal. Split 40 grand. Easy," He shrugged. "I was told to pick a gunner, so I chose Al. I planned all along to kill him myself after the Reno job. Take care of business and on the way out, put one in the back of his fucking head, and BOOM! I walk away with 40 grand all to myself."

He turned his back to Myrna, tickling underneath his chin with the barrel of the pistol.

"That is, until I got this offer. A really *enticing* offer. An offer about a *very* specific girl and a *very* specific, *very* expensive diamond necklace."

Myrna's blood ran stone cold. She felt like she could vomit. The necklace. That's what this was all about? A fucking necklace that she stole? How could this necklace even matter at this moment? She remembered how Mitch had grilled her endlessly of the whereabouts of that thing. Her one, huge mistake. Clearly, the biggest mistake of her life.

"The necklace?" Myrna asked, her throat choked with sadness. "What the fuck does that have to do with anything?"

Mitch giggled, holding the pistol with the barrel to his chin, staring her dead through the tops of his eyes.

"My boss has a vested interest in the whereabouts of said necklace. You stole it from a rich girl at your school, right? Jasmine Tolito?"

"Yeah? So?"

"Jasmine Tolito is the daughter of the head boss of the Tolito crime family," He said. He lowered his voice to a whisper. "*My* boss."

Myrna's mind fell into an endless spiral. She felt like the floor beneath her had given out, like a sink hole had opened where she knelt, swallowing her whole. She was dizzy. Drunk with sadness, confusion and endless fear. Real fear. The kind that rattles your spine. The kind that could turn your hair pure white.

Mitch began pacing yet again, his voice now at normal volume. "I had to get clearance from Mr. Tolito to kill Al, here. You don't just *kill* an employee of the Tolito family and live to talk about it. When he asked why I wanted him dead, well, I *had* to tell him. Because, another rule, you don't *lie* to the Tolito family. When he found out I had access to the girl who was accused of stealing his wife's priceless diamonds, well. He not only cleared killing Al, just for fun. But he made me a special offer for you." He pointed the gun at Myrna again.

She recoiled in fear as she stared straight down the barrel of that pistol.

"I'll, I'll give you the necklace. I don't fucking care about the diamonds. I stole it as a goof. Let's go, right now! I'll take you to them."

"No, you had your chance to give those up," He said, shaking his head. "Remember? I've asked you *multiple* times to tell me where you hid them. But no, you needed to keep that information to yourself. Your stupid, pathetic fucking game. God, you're such a child."

"I'll give them to you right now! You can take them back to the Tolitos. Please, Mitch. Please don't do this," She cried. Harder than she ever had.

"I'd really appreciate it if you told me where they are. But, it will not save you now. That time has passed. Last night, I was feeling generous. Tonight? Well," He sucked air through his teeth. "Tonight, my blood's raging, and I'm feeling mighty selfish."

"What did he offer you?" She asked, sniffling, trying to stop crying. "For me? What was the offer? What did that fucking swine promise to give you if you killed your sister? Your own flesh and blood?"

"One million up front to handle the job," He said matter-of-factly. "Two million when I prove you're *dead*. Oh, and he wants the necklace back, of course."

"So, take the fucking million and give him the necklace!" She screamed.

"I've already got the million," He said, motioning the gun towards the car, a few blocks up. "Why do you think that duffel bag never leaves my sight?"

"Jesus," Myrna said. "You've been driving around with a million dollars this entire time?"

"Yeah," He said, with a laugh so deep his shoulders bounced. "I'm a killer, Myrna. Who's gonna steal from me? Now, this is how it's gonna work. It's time for a *new* plan. From where I'm standing, it appears you broke in trying to rob poor old Al here. When you came in, a fight broke out. You stabbed him, viciously, I might add. But, before you could finish him, he got a shot or two off on you."

"You'll never get away with that," Myrna said, shaking her head.

"Oh no? Why do you think I stole his pistol from him? When they find his pistol in his hand, who's gonna question it? Before anyone is the wiser, *shit,* I'll be retired in Mexico somewhere with my two million. I'll be ankle deep in beautiful women, drunk out of my mind on the best tequila in town."

"You're willing to kill me? Your *own* sister? For two million dollars?" She screamed. "You heartless, sack of shit!"

"*Everyone* has a price, Myrna," He said, kneeling down to her level. "Two million is just enough for me to run away from this life. To forget any of this ever happened. To forget that mom, dad, hell, even to forget that *you* ever existed." He pressed the gun under her chin, lifting her head slightly. "Now, it's time to finish this. Killing makes me mighty thirsty, and I could *really* use a margarita."

CHAPTER 37

Mitch left Al's chilling body where it was, no need to move it around to stage the grisly scene. In his mind, he had fallen in a perfect spot. The fight that ensued in the living room would work perfectly for this little game to frame his sister. Now, he only needed to build the nerve to finish this. To actually *kill* his sister. The one living thing he'd always tried to protect. The girl who he carried from the house of horrors that night so many years ago, whispering to her everything would be OK. But, nothing was OK. Nothing could or would ever be OK after this night. He had reached max capacity of evil. And he was about to burst all over that house.

"Where's the mask?" Mitch asked, beginning to lose patience.

Myrna, dripping with fear, remained silent.

"The mask, god dammit," He shouted. "Where's the intruder mask?"

"I, I dropped it," She said, her voice shuddering.

"God, you didn't even follow directions properly. Coming in the house before the signal. Some natural you are. Where did you drop it?"

"In," She stuttered. "In the kitchen. On the, on the floor."

"Well, go get it. And no funny business."

Myrna crept towards the kitchen. From where she stood, she saw little no way out of this. Though, the way she saw things, it'd be better to die trying. Trying to save yourself, to save your life. By any means necessary. If you're gonna go out, you'd better go out fighting. She thought for a moment that sentiment might make her father proud. Who knows? Maybe that would've been the advice he might have given her at this moment, had he still been alive. Advice she could've used while growing up, being bullied and treated like the weird girl in town. Her entire life, she'd felt so close to her mother and father. Even if the only memories Myrna had were in fading photographs in her grandmother's dusty old photo album. Not a day went by without her hoping and praying that she somehow made them proud wherever they might be. And today, Myrna would make damn sure they'd be proud of their daughter. She'd fought all her life. And now, she'd be fighting for her life.

As she reached the kitchen, she slowly knelt to grab the mask not wanting to take her eyes off Mitch. When she did, she scanned the filthy counter tops for anything she might be able to use. Some sort of tool or sharp object that might aid her in this epic fight of fights. Al didn't keep a clean home, and it was clear he wasn't ashamed of that. The counters were littered with garbage, rotting food, filthy dishes, utensils. That was it. That would have to be it. *Utensils.* Then, she saw it. Less than an arm's length away, a filth covered fork amongst the debris. When she stood, she acted as though she'd lost her balance, using the counter top to brace herself.

"Hey, what did I tell you?" Mitch asked, his head tilted to the left. "I said no funny business. This isn't one of your bullshit horror movies where the snarky cute girl gets out alive. You can't make this go away, kid."

Myrna looked sheepishly at her feet, nodding her head in approval. What did she have to lose? Only her life. But, when push comes to shove, you'd better shove the fucker back. As she moved towards her brother, their eyes remained on one another, calculating each other's every move. It was clear his patience was all but gone as he rolled his eyes deep.

"Come *on* already!" He shouted.

"OK, OK," She said, her voice calm.

They stood for a moment, both silent. Mitch smiled at his baby sister, admiring her face, her eyes, soaking in who she was. With the back of his right hand, he brushed her soft cheek. He could feel the warm dampness from the tears that had fallen, leaving a trail of sadness in their wake.

"Kneel," He whispered.

Myrna said nothing, choosing to follow his orders precisely. She knelt below him, just in front of where Al's cold, dead feet had fallen. The stage had been set, Mitch had planned this perfectly. Frame his own sister for a robbery gone wrong. It would be open and shut, she figured. By the time the cops and paramedics arrived, Mitch would be miles from here. Safe, unharmed and stupidly rich. They'd be zipping up the black bags, stuffing their lifeless bodies into meat wagons and Mitch would be long gone. High tailing it in his luxury car towards Mexico.

"It didn't have to be this way, Myrna," He purred, lifting the pistol to her head.

"I know," She nodded. "It's my fault. I should've given you the necklace. But, before you do this. Can I say one thing?"

"What's that? You want to beg? Save yourself the trouble, kid. It's not gonna do any good. Besides, begging is so unbecoming. A little brotherly advice? Die with some dignity."

"No, no," She shook her head. "Not that. It's just, you taught me so much. How to harm, how to kill. All so I could kill *him*. And I want you to know that I listened. I really listened."

"Thank you, Myrna. You can die knowing you had my respect. Is that good enough?"

"Wait, that's not all. I just felt like I taught you some things, too. But I don't believe you ever really listened to me."

"How do you figure?"

"You taught me all those fatal kill shots. But I told you about one, too."

"I don't know what you're talking about, kid."

"That's exactly what I was banking on," She said, gritting her teeth.

From within her left sleeve, she dropped the filthy fork, the handle landing into her palm. She bellowed a guttural scream, thrusting the fork into his groin. She jumped to her feet, holding the fork in place, jamming and twisting it deeper as she went. He let out a throaty gasp, followed by an intense, high-pitched wail. Reaching for his pulverized groin with both hands, he dropped the pistol, kneeling and lurching forward, his body crashing into hers.

"You thought I was kidding about the balls," She whispered with an evil smile. "Now, you've learned something, too. You piece of shit!"

She thrust the fork upwards one last time before tearing it from his genitals. He fell to his knees, crying and whimpering, drool dripping from his lips as tears fell from his eyes. Myrna rushed to Al's side, grabbing the knife Mitch bought for her before disappearing into the darkness of the kitchen. With his left hand still holding the bleeding wound, he lifted the pistol with his right. From his knees, he pointed the pistol, firing at the doorway. *BANG! BANG! BANG!* Three shots rang out. Each one bursting through the drywall, sending plumes of powder and smoke into the air. Myrna dove behind the counter, covering her ears from the explosive shots. *Guns are way louder than I imagined,* she thought to herself. She then remembered, *The pistol holds eight rounds. Three just went off. Five more to dodge. Five more to survive the night.*

"Myrna, you fucking *bitch!*" Mitch shouted through agonizing pain, a plume of gunpowder frolicking in front of his face. When he spoke, his voice sounded labored and breathy. "I told you no games, god dammit. Now, I guess we do this shit the hard way."

He rose to his feet, staggering towards the doorway. As Myrna rose to her feet, she jumped into action running past the opening in the wall, headed deeper into the house. Just as she maneuvered past a dining table, jumping over boxes and debris littering the floor, she dove into an open doorway leading to a bedroom. *BANG! BANG!* He fired off two more shots. When she landed inside the room, she crashed onto her stomach, knocking the wind out of herself. Rolling to her back, she felt her body for any bullet holes. The blood that had doused her jumpsuit wasn't hers. *Safe,* She thought. *Two more shots done. Three to go.*

"Myrna, you can't get away," He yelled in a playful tone. "You think you're going to escape from this?"

She braced herself against the wall next to the doorjamb, taking calculated, soft breaths. Then, she closed her eyes, allowing her sense of hearing to fully kick in to know where he was, and where he'd go next. Holding the knife close to her chest, she waited for him to move closer. Mitch stopped at the dining room table, turned around, and made his way through the house down the cleaner, more open path of the main hallway. The dining room, filled with too much junk for him to climb in his current state. Hell, walking alone was tough enough. No chance he would traverse actual objects in his path after what she'd done to him and his undercarriage. He held the pistol close to his face, his finger firmly pressed on the trigger. If he saw a movement of any kind, he'd be ready to knock it dead.

"Come out, come out, wherever you are, kiddo," He sang through deep breaths.

Mitch planted his back against the wall at the end of the hall, leaning his body to look over his shoulder. A doorway sat open just in front of him, one open to the right down the hall, and to the left, an open door that led to a filthy bathroom. He pointed the gun straight ahead entering the first bedroom door. It was pitch black inside, and he squinted his eyes to survey the room. As he slowly entered, Myrna shot by behind him like a flash of lightning, dropping to her knees. She pressed the sharp edge of the blade into his upper thigh, dragging the blade across the flesh of his inner leg, slicing the artery.

"Fatal!" She screamed, jumping to her feet.

Mitch screamed in pain, grabbing at his sliced inner leg. He felt blood pouring from the wound, flooding down his pants and through his fingertips.

"Fuck!" He shouted, turning towards the hall.

He watched as Myrna reached the end of the short corridor, jumping to her right into the living room. *BANG! BANG!* Two more shots rang out, clipping the drywall, sending more white smoke into the air. *One more shot to go,* she thought to herself. *One more shot and he's all mine.*

He slunk down the hall, his left leg going completely numb. He was losing fluid and losing it quickly.

"You can't win, Myrna," He shouted. "I taught you this shit. You think you can use my own moves against me?"

Myrna stayed crouched at the end of the hall just out of sight. As he sauntered down the hall, he left a thick, smeared trail of red behind him with every step he took. His face had now turned a paler shade of white.

"You," He stuttered. "You motherfucker."

She saw his shadow inching closer and closer. There, she remained sitting on the back of her feet, the knife in her right hand, blade pointing up. When she saw he was close, she sprung from around the corner, jamming the blade deep into his stomach.

"Non fatal," She said, tearing the blade from his gut. "But it fucking *sucks,* doesn't it?"

She spun her body, moving back around the corner as Mitch cowered in pain. Both hands, pressed firmly against his abdomen, the feeling of fresh warmth trickling through his hands. He lifted the pistol, steadying it the best he could as his hands shook violently. He lunged around the corner, pulling back on the trigger, blasting off one more shot. *BANG!*

Myrna fell to the ground, landing hard on her chest. As Mitch pulled his body into the main room of the house, Myrna didn't move. Not one inch. He watched as his sister lay there, still and lifeless on that stained carpeting. Laughter burst from his lips as he dropped the gun to his side.

"I fucking told you," He said, his voice weak, light laughter drooling from his lips. "I told you I'd win." He fell back, landing hard against the wall.

Swallowing hard, he sucked in as much air as he could. He was losing blood fast, his vision beginning to blur. He still needed enough strength to set the scene for when the cops arrived. But then, he decided fuck it. Where Myrna lay now was good enough. Removing his hooded sweatshirt, he wrapped it around his thigh, pulling it tight hoping to slow the blood loss. He moved to Al, wiping the handle and trigger of the pistol on Al's bloody t-shirt, placing it in his open, right hand. Standing the best he could, he made his way to the front door. Stopping for a moment, he stared at Myrna's body laying face down on the filthy carpet. He figured that the lost shot had to have done her in. The shot had to have hit her. He didn't see any other way. He was too good at what he does, too cocky, too sure of himself. Staring at her body, lying facedown on that stained carpeting, he remembered that night 16 years ago. Visions from that night flashed in his mind of him picking up little baby Myrna, carrying her to safety, sitting on the curb, waiting for help to arrive. Now, he couldn't save her. And he had 2 million reasons he didn't want to.

"Sorry it had to end like this, sis," He said, clicking his tongue. "But like I said. *Everyone* has a price."

As he turned, reaching for the door, he heard a shuffle at his feet. Before he could look down, he felt a slash against the back of his ankle, slicing clear through his Achilles tendon. Screaming in pain, he fell to his knees, as he saw Myrna rise to her feet. The dripping knife clenched in her right hand.

"No. You can't be, I shot you."

"Nah, sorry brother. You heartless bastard. You missed," She said, smiling down at him. "Looks like you're not as good at this killing thing as you thought. The apprentice always defeats the master. You stupid fucking clown shoes."

She pulled his hair back, digging the blade deep into his neck, slicing and sawing to the left.

"Fatal," She yelled. "*No one* can survive that!"

She knelt down, stabbing into his abdomen again and again.

"Nonfatal, nonfatal," She shouted with every single stab into his body.

He fell to his back, convulsing, trembling, bleeding from everywhere at once.

She tore the jumpsuit, pulling it down to her waist before she straddled him, sitting on his chest. She jammed the knife deep into his right shoulder, once, twice, again and again. All the while shouting, "Non fatal! Non fatal! *Non fucking fatal!*"

Then, staring deep into his eyes, she pressed the tip of the knife to the left side of his chest. She pushed with all of her weight, jamming the knife through flesh, through bone, digging it straight into his heart.

"Fatal," She whispered, smiling at him. "Well, look at that. I guess I was wrong. You do have a heart after all."

She gritted her teeth, screaming at him, twisting the knife in circles as it pulverized every single valve within his still beating heart. Blood squirted and splattered her face, her chest, her hands and arms. She stood, tearing the knife from his body, allowing the liquid to drip from the blade and fall all over the carpet.

"Thanks for the lessons, brother," She said. "You saved my life tonight. But like I told you, never underestimate a strong, *bad ass* woman. Especially when she is really, *really* pissed off."

Myrna, covered from waist to head in someone else's blood, stepped out into the cool air of the morning. She sat on the top step, holding her knife in her right hand. Another night filled with death, Myrna again found herself sitting on a step, covered in blood. Though this time, she didn't have her brother there to comfort her. And for the rest of her life, she wouldn't need him to do so. Now, she had her own back. And she knew, that's all she would ever need. Now and forever. She looked up at the stars high in the sky, watching them as they twinkled. For a moment, she pretended that two of those blinking stars just might be her mom and dad, winking at her, letting her know just how absolutely proud they were of her.

CHAPTER 38

A few days later...

The Tolito house was a magnificent estate in the hills overlooking Thousand Oaks. The massive villa had cream colored outer walls, expensive Italian tiled roofs and large towers in the front holding up a round outdoor balcony that provided priceless views of the expansive front lawn and into the valley. A wide staircase led from the lawn to the front door made of expensive wood with gorgeous stained glass mounted within. The home looked like they had plucked it straight out of Italy and dropped in the Coastal California town. All was peaceful that morning at the Tolito estate. Birds chirped in the trees, water bubbled and trickled in the marble fountain out front. A gorgeous morning that only money could buy.

Then, breaking through the calm that loomed over the estate, a speeding car screeched before turning onto the home's long driveway. It stopped halfway to the house when the driver's side door shot open, and a blue duffel bag was flung onto the front lawn. Following the bag was a lit Molotov cocktail which landed on the front steps, just feet from the front door.

In an instant, gigantic men in tailored suits hurried out the front door charging towards the driveway. As they arrived on the perfectly tiled pathway out front, they saw a blue Zeus X-1 scream down the driveway towards the main road, turning right, screeching its tires as it went. The men stormed the driveway pulling handguns from their waists as they ran. The flames from the homemade bomb continued to grow higher and higher towards the spires that held the second floor deck into the air, attempting to engulf and devour the front of the home in bright orange and red flames.

Emerging from the home came Mr. Tolito himself, wearing dark gray slacks, a white striped shirt that was tucked in, and brown suspenders. The look on his face was anything but calm. He was distraught, anxious and more so than anything else, he was furious. A look of death floating within his dark eyes. The armed men surrounded him as he approached the blue duffel bag as more men tended the growing flames, doing everything in their power to extinguish the blaze. The men guarding Mr. Tolito looked in all directions trying to get an eye on anyone if they tried to make a move towards their boss. Mr. Tolito knelt in the grass, unzipping the bag. From within, he removed a silver revolver, the letters A and L stamped in gold along the barrel. Next to it was a polaroid photo. He held it into the sunlight, admiring the photograph taking in everything that it showed. The story it told him. The photograph was of that same blue duffel bag filled with wrapped wads of cash. Sitting on top of the cash proudly on full display was the diamond necklace that was taken from his home. Under the photo, scribbled in sharpie it read -

Thanks for the money, asshole.

Under those words was an arrow pointing to the right. A not-so-subtle way of informing him to flip the picture over. On the back, in the same scribbled handwriting it said -

Courtesy of the Black Parade, bitch!

He crumpled the photo in his hand, his face reaching a fever pitch of fury. He clenched his teeth and bellowed, his face pointed towards the clouds. Standing to his feet, he reached for the man closest to him, grabbing hold of his collar, pulling him so close their faces touched. He was seething, his chest pumping in and out rapidly.

"Trovalo e uccidilo," Mr. Tolito screamed. *"Trovalo e uccidilo!"*

The man stared at him, a look of confusion on his face. Mr. Tolito rolled his eyes in frustration.

"Find him, you idiot!" He screamed. "Find him and kill him!"

The men tucked their guns in their respective waistbands and took off towards two cars parked on the stone driveway, three armed men entering each vehicle. As they tore down the driveway to the main road, a soft breeze blew through the surrounding trees. And in the breeze, if you listened close enough, you could almost hear the soft, subtle piano from Myrna's favorite song *Welcome to the Black Parade* floating along with it. In the distance, if you concentrated hard enough, one might have even heard the faintest whisper as the lyrics kicked in. The melody swirled along with the wind, like a mass of angry butterflies fluttering along with the breeze. Just when you'd imagine the drums kicking in, the two cars screeched out of the driveway, each taking a hard right, speeding down the main road.

Down the street, those two cars came to a dead stop when they found the blue Zeus X-1 crashed on the side of the road. It had fallen nose first into a ditch, the driver's side door hanging wide open. As the men pulled over, they pounced on the car at once, each with a gun drawn. They searched the car, finding no one inside. Next to the ditch was a large field littered with trees. It stretched deep alongside the Tolito estate, trees and brush as far as the eye could see.

"He ran through the trees! Come on, let's go!" One man yelled, storming down the ditch, gun drawn, disappearing into the woods.

The other men, all but one, rushed through the trees looking for Mitch. The man Tolito figured ripped him off for a cool million dollars and his wife's prized necklace. No one was ever to steal from the Tolito family. If one did, it was punishable by death. Now, Tolito only had one person on his radar. His loyal gunman, Mitch Graves. Tolito would go to the end of the Earth to get what he wanted. Now, more than anything, he wanted Mitch's head on a spike in his front yard.

One man remained outside the trees and weeds, leering over his left shoulder watching the road. His eyes remained stuck on the road as a black car lurched slowly towards him. He kept his eyes on that car as though it mesmerized him. There he stayed until another one of Tolito's men grabbed him by the arm.

"Come on!" He urged. "Don't just stand there! He ran into the trees!"

"OK, OK," The man agreed, rushing towards the woods following the others.

As the black car got closer, the breeze picked up even more. It blew through the trees, shaking branches as it passed. Birds burst from hidden nests, taking flight, as though the song Myrna loved with all her heart was still swirling within the wind blowing through the branches and the leaves. And just about where the drum roll kicked in on Myrna's favorite song, accompanied by the searing guitar solo, a shiny, black hearse passed the Zeus X-1. The paint was pristine, the glass crystal clear. On the back windows, merlot colored drapes hung, matching the beautiful interior. Behind the wheel, driving the massive beast was Myrna, screaming, cheering and dancing in her seat as the song hit the first high point. She pressed the gas pedal deep into the floorboards, picking up immense speed as the hearse shot past the Tolito residence.

She reached for the glove box, removing a bootleg cassette tape with *The Black Parade* scribbled in black ink. She shoved it into the tape deck, pressing play, cranking the volume as high as the speakers could handle. Lifting her cell phone from the center console, she immediately began pounding away at the touch screen, texting her best friend, Deidre.

Pack a bag bitch, we're going to Jersey. Pick you up in 30. MCR Tix on me! It's time to start our summer! The text read, followed by three black flag emojis.

She pressed send, dropping the phone onto the passenger seat. A wild smile grew on her face as she gripped the wheel with all her strength, screaming into the air as her knuckles turned white. On the passenger seat was her backpack, the same one she'd had with her the entire, fateful trip. She unzipped it, reached in, and amongst the countless wads of crisp hundred-dollar bills, she removed the diamond necklace. The mass of diamonds sent shimmering flashes all over the inside of the hearse as she fashioned it around her neck. She admired herself proudly in the rear-view mirror. At that moment, there wasn't much that she loved more than how the gold and diamonds accented her pitch black hair, dark makeup and the way it rested just perfectly over the Misfits logo on her t-shirt. It was fitting. Somehow, it worked. Beautifully gothic. Tough as nails. Punk as fuck. As *the Black Parade* played loudly within the hearse, the breeze carried the tune along with her as she drove that beautiful machine towards the horizon. She knew then, no matter what the world threw her way, she'd always carry on. Nothing and no one could ever take her down. And eventually, when someone would try again, she'd always remember to keep marching on. It was finally time to start her summer. And what a fucking summer it would be.

ACKNOWLEDGEMENTS

Thank You to Tabitha for always supporting whatever wild idea I may come up with and always being my number one fan. Thanks for always pushing me to keep working no matter how beat down I may feel. Thank You to Wilma, Rufus, Sidney, Griff and Lemmy Rose for showing unconditional love at all times. Thank You to my entire family for always being there for me, no matter how hard I have made it at. Thank You for being you, and for loving me for me, always.

A huge Thank You and many High Fives for - Hannah for being such an amazing editor to work with. Your knowledge and expertise were paramount and I owe you infinitely. JulieAnne, Matthew and Stormy, The Servis and Gelsomino families, Raylee for the laughs and believing in me. The entire Oasis Beer Club Family. Duddy, Steve, Bill, (evil) Matt, Mike, Noah and Thomas for being true brothers through it all. A huge LETS GET IT to Jeff and the Ice Cream Posse family as well as to Chris and Little Ghost Books. Also, The Golden State Warriors and San Diego Padres. Get those rings. A Special Thank You goes out to Aquino Loayza, Lor Gislason and Erica Robyn for reading this book early and providing cover blurbs. It means the world. Also, massive shout out and all the love to My Chemical Romance for providing 600+ hours of listening pleasure as I wrote this story. Without that music, the story of Myrna and Mitch may have never come to life.

Thank You to Reagan and the Black Rose Family for making this dream a reality. I will forever be indebted to your trust, confidence and dedication to the craft. And to anyone who bought, found, borrowed and read this book. Thank You, Thank You, THANK YOU. You have contributed, knowingly or not, in making a dream come true. And for that, I will be forever thankful.

To anyone and everyone out there with a dream - Get out and make it happen. Don't ever let anyone tell you what you can or can't do. Let nothing stand in your way. The book you are currently holding in your hands is proof that dreams can come true. Now, go make yours happen. And to anyone who feels or has ever felt unseen or unheard - May the brightest, most beautiful light shine upon you and allow the world to see how truly amazing you are. You got this. Lets Get it!

If you gave this story a chance, Thank You. Much Love, Always.

ABOUT THE AUTHOR

Cody J. Thompson is a horror writer from San Diego, California. His two previous horror novels *Bone Saw Serenade* and *This One's Gonna Hurt* were published in 2022 and 2023. He has written for numerous magazines and newspapers throughout Southern California and in 2023 had a story featured in a horror anthology. When he is not writing or reading he spends time with his wife and their three pit bulls while cheering for his Golden State Warriors and San Diego Padres. He hates the hiccups and loves Galaga. Follow Cody on social media @CodyWritesBooks.

OTHER TITLES BY CODY J. THOMPSON

Note from Cody J. Thompson

Word-of-mouth is crucial for any author to succeed. If you enjoyed *Find Him and Kill Him*, please leave a review online—anywhere you are able. Even if it's just a sentence or two. It would make all the difference and would be very much appreciated.

Thanks!
Cody J. Thompson

We hope you enjoyed reading this title from:

BLACK&ROSE
writing™

www.blackrosewriting.com

Subscribe to our mailing list – *The Rosevine* – and receive **FREE** books, daily deals, and stay current with news about upcoming releases and our hottest authors.
Scan the QR code below to sign up.

Already a subscriber? Please accept a sincere thank you for being a fan of Black Rose Writing authors.

View other Black Rose Writing titles at www.blackrosewriting.com/books and use promo code **PRINT** to receive a **20% discount** when purchasing.